Ellen's Book of Life

Ellen's Book of Life

Joan Givner

GROUNDWOOD BOOKS
HOUSE OF ANANSI PRESS
TORONTO BERKELEY

I thank Merrill Joan Gerber and Elizabeth Brewster for their suggestions. As always, I am immensely grateful to my editor, Shelley Tanaka, for the great expertise and sensitivity she brings to my work.

Published in Canada and the USA in 2008 by Groundwood Books

Groundwood Books / House of Anansi Press
110 Spadina Avenue, Suite 801, Toronto, Ontario M5V 2K4
or c/o Publishers Group West
1700 Fourth Street, Berkeley, CA 94710

We acknowledge for their financial support of our publishing program the Canada Council for the Arts, the Government of Canada through the Book Publishing Industry Development Program (BPIDP) and the Ontario Arts Council.

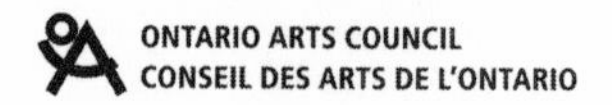

Library and Archives Canada Cataloguing in Publication
Givner, Joan
Ellen's book of life / Joan Givner.
ISBN-13: 978-0-88899-853-8 (bound).–
ISBN-10: 0-88899-853-8 (bound).–
ISBN-13: 978-0-88899-860-6 (pbk.).–
ISBN-10: 0-88899-860-0 (pbk.)–
I. Title.
PS8563.I86E458 2008 jC813'.54 C2008-902514-8

Cover illustration by Karine Daisay
Design by Michael Solomon
Printed and bound in Canada

To the memory of
Emily Givner
and her grandmothers,
Ann Givner and Elizabeth Short

1

I WAS STARTLED when I heard my name on the morning announcements, even though it was just a message that Mr. Higginson wanted to see me at lunch. Higg is my favorite teacher, but I was a little worried all the same. I tried to remember if I'd mouthed off at one of the teachers lately. Higg was always warning me about that.

"Oh, there you are, Ellen," he said when I walked in. "Do you still have a copy of that speech you gave on vegetarianism?"

"I think so," I said.

"Well, I'd like you to give it at the provincial debating tournament."

"The Provincials!" I said. "Don't you have to be older?"

"Generally you do," he said. "But our contestant in the public-speaking contest at the novice level has just dropped out. I'd like you to take her place."

"Isn't it in Vancouver?"

"That's no problem. I'll give you a ride over there."

"When is it?"

"Next weekend. We'd go over on Friday and come back the next day. You'd be billeted overnight with one of the Vancouver debaters."

"I can't do it," I said.

I wasn't worried about the contest. I like giving speeches, but Mum's illness had got a lot worse in the past year. She was in bed all the time now and she needed me to do certain jobs for her.

"Sure you can, Ellen. It'll be good experience."

"It's not the speech," I said. "It's Mum."

"I thought you had home care. And doesn't Kelly help out?"

"Yes, but I'm the one that gets Mum ready for bed at night."

"Suppose I get you there and back the same day? We could do that if we leave first thing Saturday morning. The public-speaking contest is after lunch. Would you be able to go then?"

"I guess," I said.

So that was how I ended up at the debating tournament.

I didn't get nervous ahead of time because I was too busy. It was when we got to the big Vancouver high school that my heart sank right down into my sneakers. Higg left me in the cafeteria while he went to register and get my name tag. The place was full of kids laughing and talking with each other. I got some orange juice out of a machine and sat in a corner by myself drinking it and watching them.

They were all older than me and they were all dressed up. The girls had matching tops and pants, and a few were wearing dresses. The boys wore blazers or suits, and some of them even carried briefcases.

Then I heard someone say my name. I was so startled that the juice went all down the front of my T-shirt.

It was Jon Davidson, one of the best debaters at our school. All his friends called him Spotz. He lived on Partridge Cove Road and he sometimes walked home from school with us. I liked him a lot because he made me feel better one time when I got down on myself after a speech contest.

"Wow! Are you ever jumpy!" he said. "Are you okay?"

"I think so," I said. "I'm a bit scared. Will there be a lot of people in the audience?"

"Probably," he said, "but don't worry. Just look at Higg and pretend you're at school having a rehearsal. You could straighten your hair up a bit, though. And maybe try and get that juice off the front of your shirt."

I felt even worse when we went to the room where the contest was being held. It was a big auditorium and it was filling up with students and their parents. There was a platform at the front with a speaker's podium on one side, and a table with a water jug, glasses and a silver cup facing it on the other. Between them was a long row of chairs.

When the room was nearly full, two people walked up to the platform. One was a small woman with frizzy hair, wearing a black pantsuit. She sat down at the table and started taking papers out of her briefcase.

The other was a friendly-looking man who went to the podium and welcomed us. Then he introduced the judge. He said we were honored to have her with us because she'd just won a big case before the Supreme Court of Canada. She'd flown back from Ottawa overnight just to keep her commitment to the debating tournament. The audience clapped and the judge nodded but didn't smile. Her hair was pretty messy and she tried to push it behind her ears.

Then he asked the contestants to come up to the platform. I sat in the middle of the row and I was the only one wearing jeans and a T-shirt. When we were all seated, he read out the name of the first contestant.

She was tall and pretty, and she was wearing a skirt, a black velvet jacket and black shoes with heels. She gave a good speech about training guide dogs for blind people, but a bell rang before she was finished.

The next speaker was a boy wearing a suit. He'd completely memorized his speech and didn't look down once at his notes.

I was the fifth speaker. When I heard my name, I walked to the podium and pulled my cards out of my back pocket. My hands were shaking as I took the rubber band off them. Then I remembered what Spotz had said, and I looked at Higg. He was in the second row, and he gave me a big smile and a thumbs-up sign.

The judge scribbled away the whole time we were speaking and she went on scribbling for a while after we'd finished. Finally she gathered her notes up and walked across to the podium. She made some general remarks about timing and eye contact and stuff like that. Then she started to criticize the speakers one by one.

When it was my turn, she glared at me for a moment before she spoke.

"A public-speaking contest, like a debate or a court appearance, is a formal occasion," she said. "It requires participants to dress appropriately. Not to do so indicates a lack of respect for the audience, for your fellow contestants, and for the judge. Blue jeans and a T-shirt do not constitute appropriate dress."

Everyone was staring at me, and suddenly the room got very quiet. I looked down and saw the orange juice stain on my T-shirt. I'd put water on it in the washroom, but it hadn't come off.

I could feel my face getting red. I wanted to jump off the platform and run down the aisle and out the door.

I thought how Higg had talked me into coming all the way to Vancouver when I didn't want to, and how Mum needed me at home, and how I hadn't had time to get any proper clothes.

Then the boy next to me gave a loud laugh. It made me so mad I completely lost it.

"I didn't have a lack of respect," I said. "I had a lack of time. I got roped into this contest at the last minute because somebody else dropped out and I didn't even want to be — "

Just then I caught sight of Higg. His face was as red as mine, and he was shaking his head from side to side. I got the message, shut up and sat down. I couldn't wait to get out of there.

After she'd done enough criticizing, the judge went back to the table and announced the winners. She started with the third-place winner. The boy who'd laughed got that. He went to collect it and shook the judge's hand. It was some kind of certificate with a gold seal. Then there was the second-place winner. The girl in the velvet jacket got that. As she walked to the table a flashbulb went off in the audience. I guess her mum or dad wanted a picture of her.

Then the judge called, "Ellen Fremedon."

I was so surprised, I didn't move. The laughing boy stuck his elbow in my ribs.

"That's you," he said.

The judge was holding up the silver cup. She handed it to me, but she looked as if she'd rather not shake my hand. The friendly man shook my hand a bit too much, pumping it up and down.

"That was wonderful, Ellen," he said, smiling at me. "I hope you get roped in again next year."

Fat chance, I thought.

Everyone in the audience clapped, and then they started filing out of the room. Some of them said congratulations when I walked by. One man said, "Great speech, kiddo!"

"I don't know whether to pat you on the back or wring your neck," Higg said, but he looked pretty pleased.

"Do you think I won because I was the youngest in my category?" I asked Higg later. We were on the ferry and he'd got me a cheeseburger with a side of fries.

"You won because you gave the best speech," Higg said. "Didn't you hear what the judge said about you being a forceful speaker? She said you made excellent points and set them out in a very logical progression."

"I wasn't listening," I said. "I was too mad at what she said about my clothes."

"I was sure you'd blown it when you started talking back to her," Higg said. "Never, ever, argue with a judge."

"Well, she shouldn't have chewed me out. It's not how you look, it's how smart you are. Besides, she wasn't one to talk. Did you see her hair?"

"She'd been sitting in a plane all night. Maybe your explanation rang a bell with her. Anyway, she didn't hold it against you in the long run. But don't pull anything like that again next year."

When I got home, the light was still on in Mum's room, so I went in and showed her my trophy

"That's marvelous," she said. "I'm so proud of you. Tell me everything that happened."

So I sat on the edge of her bed and told her about the mean judge, the boy who laughed at me, and the girl in the velvet jacket. I told her I'd talked to Spotz in the cafeteria.

Mum is the only person who knows I like him, and how much I'm going to miss him when he moves to Vancouver this summer. I can tell her things I can't tell anyone else in the world, not even my best friend, Jenny.

"We should have warned you about dressing a bit more formally," she said.

"It wouldn't have made any difference," I said, "because I don't have any dressy clothes."

"No, you don't, do you?" she said. She looked sad.

"It doesn't matter," I said. "I hate getting dressed up. Besides, I won anyway."

She looked very tired suddenly and her eyes were drooping, so I kissed her good night and tiptoed out of the room. I left the trophy on the bedside table so that she'd see it when she woke up in the morning.

2

THE DAY AFTER school got out for the summer, Jenny and I were in Somecot. That's short for Something Cottage. It's the converted potting shed that's my own private place at the bottom of our garden. Jenny's very keen on fixing it up. Her mum's an interior decorator, so I guess it runs in the blood. She was just finishing a shelf to hang on the wall for my trophy.

"Maybe a red backing would show off the trophy better," she said.

"It looks great the way it is," I said.

"I'll make it bigger if you win another trophy next year," she said.

"Yeah, right." Next year seemed a long way off

when there was the whole summer stretching ahead of us.

Normally the end of the school year is a real bummer for me. Our family can't take holidays because of Mum, so usually I'm stuck in Partridge Cove while Jenny goes off to an art camp in Saskatchewan.

But this summer was going to be different. I'd been invited to Toronto to spend a month with Dimsie Fairchild and her mother. I met Dimsie last summer when she was visiting her grandmother in Partridge Cove. I made friends with her whole family, and her grandmother, Mrs. Broster, had been my music teacher for the past year. Dimsie's mum's a concert pianist, and she was going to take us to a lot of concerts and museums and art galleries.

Jenny and I were going to fly from the Victoria airport together and change planes in Calgary. Then she'd take a flight to Regina and I'd take one to Toronto.

"I wish you were going to an art school in Toronto so we could fly the whole way together," I said. "I'm a bit nervous about changing planes and flying to Toronto by myself."

For the past week my little twin brothers had been going on about all the terrible things that would happen if I got on the wrong plane by mistake.

"The biggest danger in foreign countries is spiders," Tim said.

He'd got a book about spiders out of the library and he kept reading aloud about various kinds of venom. The most dangerous spider was the tarantula. It was named for the town of Taranto in Italy where there were a lot of them. If it bit you, you could go mad or die.

"If you end up in Italy and get bitten, you have to dance for weeks until the venom comes out of your pores in your sweat. That's the only cure," Toby said.

"You guys have spiders on the brain," I said.

Normally Dad tells the twins to knock it off when they start getting too stupid, but lately he didn't seem to hear anything that was going on around him. Half the time he didn't even eat with us. He carried his food into Mum's room and sat beside her bed eating it.

"Do you worry about getting on the wrong plane?" I asked Jenny.

"Of course not," Jenny said. "It's not like the bus station in the city with all the buses lined up. They check your ticket and give you a boarding pass. You couldn't get on the wrong plane if you tried. The thing you have to worry about is getting packed. You haven't even started yet, have you?"

"I have to get some stuff out of the washer and put it in the dryer before I start packing," I said.

"You'd better do it right away," she said, "because we'll be picking you up at seven in the morning. We have to be at the airport two hours before our flight leaves."

Jenny had to do some last-minute shopping, so I went back to the house. Kelly, who was our full-time caregiver last year, was only coming in part-time because she was taking a course in summer school. She wasn't there and Dad and the twins were out, so I made lunch for Mum and me.

I fixed myself a cheese sandwich in a pita pocket. Then I made a really nice salad for Mum. She didn't have much appetite since she stayed in bed all the time, so I tried to make it as tempting as possible. I arranged slices of avocado and cucumber in a circle on a bed of lettuce with cherry tomatoes and radishes. Then I sliced a hard-boiled egg, mixed the yolks with mayonnaise and chopped parsley and scooped the mixture back into the halves. I put it all on a tray and carried it into Mum's bedroom.

Since she'd been bedridden, Mum needed a lot

of help. I kept the vases in her room full of fresh flowers, changed their water, put them on the table outside her door after I helped her get ready for bed at night, and took them back in the morning. I collected her mail and newspapers and took in her meals and medicines.

When I carried in her lunch tray she put down the letter she was reading.

"Why, that's beautiful, Ellen," she said when she saw the salad. "What have you been doing all morning?"

I told her about the trophy shelf Jenny had made.

"You really ended the school year on a high note, didn't you?" she said. "Top marks in all your subjects, and then winning the trophy! And Mrs. Broster says you're doing very well at your music. I'm so proud of you."

"How will you get along without me when I'm away?" I said.

"I'll manage very well," she said. "It's only for a month and the twins have promised to do the flowers."

"They don't do everything they promise," I said.

"I think they will this time. I'm giving them a quarter every time they change my flowers. They're saving up for a tarantula and I have a feeling this room will look like a flower shop by the time you get home."

"But you'll miss me, won't you?" I said

"I'll miss you a whole lot, Ellen," she said, holding my hand. "But I'm looking forward to your trip almost as much as you are. You know how much I love getting letters."

It was true. Reading her mail was the high point of Mum's day. She got tons of letters and cards. Dimsie said I could use her laptop while I was in Toronto, and Dad had promised to print out the messages and take them into Mum. I intended to write two or three times a day and tell her what we were doing.

"Don't you like your salad?" I said. I'd finished my sandwich, but all Mum had eaten was half a cherry tomato.

"It's almost too pretty to eat," she said. "Have you finished packing?"

"I'll finish it this afternoon. I have to do some laundry first," I said.

For a while I watched her push the slices of avocado and cucumber around with her fork, but she didn't eat them.

"This is rather a lot for one person," she said. "Why don't you help me out? I think I can manage half a deviled egg, if you'll eat the other half."

She took a bite out of half an egg and I ate the other half.

"Don't you like it?" I asked.

"You don't need as much food when you aren't active," she said. So I ended up eating most of her lunch as well as my own.

"Ellen," she said, when I was gathering up the tray, "if Dad asks, don't tell him I didn't eat much lunch. He tends to worry too much."

"He probably won't ask."

"Be sure to say goodbye to me before you go to bed tonight," she said. "You might be in too much of a rush in the morning."

"I always come in to put your flowers out," I said.

"Yes, you do, Ellen," she said. "You're very conscientious."

The first thing Dad asked when he and the twins came back was if Mum had eaten a good lunch.

"I made her a salad," I said.

"Yes, but did she eat it?"

"She ate some of it."

He sighed.

The twins were reading a flyer they'd got from the pet store in the village. It was for NEW REPTILE ARRIVALS and ALL BIRDS 30% OFF. Most of the reptiles and birds were fairly cheap, but the twins didn't want them, or the turtles or toads. They wanted a tarantula with hairy legs.

"You'd better start learning to dance," I said, "because if it bites you, you'll be doing a lot of it. Maybe I'll accompany you on the piano."

"The ones in the store don't bite," Tim said. "They're pets."

There were three kinds advertised. The Rosehair was $30, the Tiger Rump was $68.99, and the one they really wanted—the Mexican Beauty—was $129.99. And this was without the cage to keep it in.

They sat down and started adding up numbers on a piece of paper. They were trying to work out how many times they'd have to change the flowers in Mum's room before they could buy the Mexican Beauty.

"It's not just the cost," I said. "You'll have to buy food for it, too."

"No, we won't," Tim said. "It eats crickets, but we can catch them ourselves. They have to be alive. It won't go after them unless it sees them moving. But its mouth can only suck food up, so when it catches bugs it has to squish them into juice before it can—"

"Yuck!" I said.

I didn't want to share my living quarters with a disgusting tarantula, even if it was in a cage and it wasn't poisonous. But at least Mum would get all the help she needed for the next month.

When I went in to say good night, Mum gave me an envelope with a bunch of twenty-dollar bills in it.

"Dad's already given me some money," I said.

"This is for extras," she said. "You're sure to see a lot of things you want to buy in the city."

I was so excited about my trip that I forgot to take out Mum's flowers. When I left the next morning I noticed they weren't on the table outside her room. They must have been in there all night, sucking up all her oxygen and filling the air with nasty carbon dioxide.

3

I ACTUALLY DIDN'T write home two or three times a day when I was in Toronto, because I was too busy. But I did send Mum one long e-mail every morning. It wasn't hard to write because I had so much stuff to tell her.

We couldn't go out as often as we'd planned because Catriona was going to have a baby soon, and she didn't feel well. One night at supper we tried to think of names for the new baby. It was going to be a girl, and Catriona and I thought a musical name would be nice, like Minuetta or Allegra or Cadenza. Dimsie said it wasn't fair to give a kid a name that needed explaining to everyone. She thought a plain name like Sue or Jane or Ellen would be better.

I didn't mind not going out because their house was so nice. They had a swimming pool and two grand pianos, and Dimsie even had a TV in her room. She had tons of DVDs, and we watched them after we went to bed. Catriona didn't care how late we stayed up because there was no school the next day. So we watched until we fell asleep and slept late the next morning.

One day when Catriona was feeling okay, she took us downtown. The next morning I sat down with Dimsie's laptop and started a letter to Mum.

Dear Mum,
I hope the twins are doing a good job with your flowers. Catriona said it wasn't a problem that I'd forgotten to pack any socks and underwear. I borrowed some of Dimsie's, also her PJs.

Then yesterday Catriona took us shopping. We drove to the Eaton Centre where they have a million stores. You can get much nicer stuff than they have at the Clothes Loft and it's a lot cheaper. I got three pairs of socks for five dollars. I used the money you gave me. Then Catriona bought us three pairs of really super ones because we'd cleaned up the kitchen yesterday. I got ones with frogs on them, tell the twins. After that we went to the art gallery and had lunch there.

I was just going to tell Mum what I'd seen in the art gallery, when Catriona slipped into the room very quietly. She sat on the chair beside me at the computer, took my hand and held it in both of hers.

"Ellen, dear," she said. "I have some sad news, or disappointing, rather..."

"What is it?"

"I'm afraid you're going to have to go home."

My first thought was that they were sending me away because I'd turned out to be too much trouble. I'm awfully clutzy and that morning I'd spilled juice on the tablecloth. I'd also broken a glass when Dimsie and I were unloading the dishwasher the night before.

Then I thought maybe Catriona was ill, or her baby was coming early, because her face was so pale.

"Don't you feel well?" I said.

"It isn't me," she said. "It's your mother. Oh, honey, I'm so sorry. But I do promise you'll come back another time, and we'll do all the things we planned."

"When?" I said. "Later this summer?"

"Come back whenever you'd like."

Then Dimsie came into the room, and I could see she'd been crying. They both treated me like I was sick instead of Mum. Catriona explained that Mum had been rushed to the hospital and that Dad wanted me home immediately.

"How can I go home?" I said. "My return ticket isn't for another three weeks."

They told me that Dimsie's dad had already changed my ticket and got me on a direct flight to Victoria.

I pressed the Send button on my letter before I realized that Mum wouldn't be at home to read it.

After that, it was all a blur because I had to get my stuff together in a hurry. Dimsie helped me pack and her dad came back from his office to drive me to the airport. I'd been in Toronto less than a week and there I was back on the plane going home. My beautiful holiday was ruined.

There's plenty of time to think when you're sitting in an airplane for five hours and all you can see out the window is clouds. There was a movie on a screen in front but it didn't look interesting, and I didn't put the headphones on.

After a while, I stopped thinking about my ruined summer and started worrying about Mum. She takes an awful lot of different pills, and you have to be very careful when you count them out. I wondered if Kelly and Dad had got too busy and forgotten the pills or got them mixed up. Maybe that was why Mum had to be rushed to the hospital. They probably realized they'd need extra help when she got home, and so they'd sent for me. They didn't care about my holiday. It was less important than Kelly's summer school course and the stupid book Dad was working on.

I was expecting Dad to meet me when I got off the plane in Victoria. There was a crowd of people waiting. Then I saw Jenny's mother, Anne, and her partner, Cathy Banks, at the front of the crowd. They both waved when they saw me, but neither of them smiled. I figured they weren't too thrilled at being asked to make a round trip to the airport when they were just about to have their supper.

"Where's my dad?" I said, while we waited to get my bags off the carousel. "Why didn't he come and get me?"

"Ellen, dear, your dad and your grandmother are still at the hospital," Anne said. "Kelly's looking after the twins."

"When are they bringing Mum home?" I said after we got in the car.

Cathy just looked out the window, concentrating on the road. Anne was in the back seat and when I looked around I could see she was dabbing her face with a tissue. Neither of them answered my question.

Then it suddenly hit me why Catriona had looked so pale, and why Dimsie had been crying, and why Anne and Cathy weren't smiling. I knew without anyone telling me that my mother was never going to get out of the hospital, and that I'd never see her again.

All I could think of as we drove home was Mum telling me to say goodbye the night before my trip because I'd be in too much of a rush in the morning. I remembered the empty table outside her room the morning I left. I wondered if sleeping in a room full of flowers could poison a person who was already really sick.

"I should never have gone away," I said. "Why did my dad let me go away?" I was shouting.

"Oh, Ellen, he didn't know this was going to happen so soon," Cathy said. "No one expected it."

"Don't be mad at your dad, Ellen, dear," Anne said. "He's got enough on his plate just now. You must try to help him."

"Why don't you come home with us tonight?" Cathy said. "You can sleep in Jenny's room."

"I don't want to come home with you and sleep

in Jenny's room," I said. "I want to sleep in my own bed."

When we got to our house, Cathy carried my suitcase up to the door and put it on the step. She looked as if she wanted to hug me so I pushed past her quickly. I didn't even say thank you for the ride.

I opened the door and dumped my bags on the floor inside. As I was closing the door, I looked outside. I saw that Cathy hadn't started the car. Anne had moved to the front seat and they were both sitting there just staring at the house.

4

THE MEMORIAL SERVICE for Mum was a celebration of her life. That was what it said on the brochures Anne and Cathy had made.

ELINOR FREMEDON

A CELEBRATION OF HER LIFE

"The Glory of the Garden it abideth not in words."

The brochures were on a table by the door so that people could pick one up after they signed the guest book.

I don't know whose idea it was to call it a celebration. I didn't think we had much to celebrate. We all knew Mum was ill because she'd had MS for a long time, but I still thought she'd always be there, listening to my problems, giving me advice and laughing at Dad's dumb jokes. Then suddenly she wasn't there any more. The service was supposed to make us feel better, but it just made me feel a whole lot worse.

The only person who felt better was Gran.

"It was a beautiful service. Elinor would have loved it," she said. "And the hall was jam-packed. Not an empty seat in that whole place."

That was true. It seemed like everybody in Partridge Cove had turned out, whether they knew Mum or not. I don't know who invited them and, of course, nobody asked me who should come. I couldn't figure out why people who hadn't seen Mum for years thought they had any right to be there. Maybe they came for the refreshments.

It was held in the community hall, and someone had stuck photographs on easels all around the stage. They didn't look like Mum at all, at least not the way I knew her. They were pictures of her as a girl and then a young woman. But she'd been sick for so long, I felt like she'd been in a wheelchair forever.

Some lady played the harp, Mrs. Broster played the piano, and Higg read a poem by Robert Frost. It was about some lady who looked like a silken tent in a field on a summer day. I didn't get it. Mum didn't look like a tent. Then a lot of people got up and told stories about how Mum had given them advice or plants or cured the blight on their roses. It seemed like they were all talking about someone I didn't know.

Dad got up last. He had a speech written out and he read it with a glum face like he was giving a boring lecture in one of his philosophy classes at the university. He said how proud Mum was of her children and that she had a good life and a rich enjoyment of her garden and her books and everything. But we all knew she hadn't had a rich enjoyment of her garden because she couldn't even get down there. She looked at it through the window and it made her sad because she wanted to be on her knees digging and planting.

Afterwards there were refreshments. Anne and Cathy arranged it and people brought tons of sandwiches and stuff. All the speeches must have made them hungry because they started gobbling up the food. Tim and Toby ran off home because they didn't like being kissed by old ladies.

Jenny came up to me as soon as all the neighbors got through telling me how sorry they were for me. I'd spotted her when our family had walked up to the front row after everybody was seated. I was really surprised because she still had two months to go at the summer school for the arts.

"What are you doing here?" I said. "You're supposed to be at art camp."

"I came back early," she said.

"What for?"

"I thought maybe you'd want me to," she said.

"Well, I don't."

I was awfully mean to Jenny after the memorial service.

I spent a lot of time by myself, mostly walking down to the Partridge Cove marina. I walked along the wooden ramps where the boats were moored. It's a very rundown marina with a lot of broken planks. If you don't watch out you could put your foot through the holes. Farther out, the mother seals and their pups lay sunning themselves. I walked nearer and nearer to them so that I scared them and they flopped into the water with a splash. When I'd disturbed them all, I turned back and went along the beach.

I walked close to the shoreline where the seaweed and shells get washed up after the tide goes out. A lot of baby crabs are left stranded. I stepped on as many as I could, and killed them.

"Sorry, crabs!" I said.

It felt good stomping on the tiny crabs. They'd

never have made it anyway, lying there in the hot sun until the next high tide.

I never lock the door of Somecot. So often while I was out walking, Jenny left things on my desk. I'd come in and find a book, or a chocolate bar, or a card with one of her origami cranes stuck on it. Sometimes there'd be a note saying she hoped I was feeling better, and why didn't we go and get some ice cream and would I call her.

I dropped everything in the wastebasket she'd given me as a present the first year Mum and Dad got Somecot fixed up for me.

It was Mum's idea to turn the old potting shed into a little house so that I'd have a private room of my own away from the twins. I put the waste-basket where Jenny was sure to see it. I bet she wished she'd stayed in Saskatchewan at the art camp.

Gran came up on Sundays as usual, and the lunches were terrible because Tim kept crying and saying he missed Mum. Dad was super nice to Gran, even though she said a lot of things that would normally drive him up the wall. She said Mum had gone to a better place.

"Let's hope so, Mother," he said.

"What's it like in the better place?" Tim said.

Gran said Mum was in heaven with her father

who'd been a great gardener. She knew they were sitting side by side in their armchairs talking about their gardens. Mum would be telling him about her flowers and Grandad would be telling Mum about his vegetables.

She went on and on like this, and Dad didn't try to stop her, even though he doesn't believe in religion, and doesn't like people telling us a lot of stuff that's not true. Now it seemed he didn't care whether anybody talked nonsense, just like he didn't care whether we ate right, or ate anything at all. He didn't even care how he looked. He had on a crummy old sweater he wore all the time, and it had stains all down the front where he'd slurped his coffee and soup.

Tim asked Gran if Mum would be in her wheelchair in heaven. Gran said all the sick and injured people would be healed in heaven. Mum would no longer need her wheelchair because she'd have regained the use of her legs. Tim said he was going to kill himself so he could end up in heaven.

"How would you do that?" I said. "You blubber like crazy when you get a shot at the clinic."

"I'll climb on the roof and jump off."

"You'll just end up with a broken ankle and cause Dad a lot of trouble and expense."

Gran said she could feel Mum's presence when she walked in the garden.

"What part of the garden?" Toby said.

"Every part."

"Even by the compost heap where it stinks?"

"The compost heap shouldn't smell bad unless somebody's been throwing things on it that have no business being there," Gran said. "Elinor and I had differing views on keeping compost heaps."

You're telling me! They had differing views on everything, but Gran seemed to have forgotten all about that.

Then Gran went on about how close she and Mum were.

"For many years there were just the two of us," she said. "So we were closer than most mothers and daughters. She was fond of teasing me, of course. Especially about my weakness for hats. But we never had a cross word. She had a wonderful temperament."

I wished she wouldn't keep saying stuff like that, because the look on Dad's face wasn't just the look he gets when she says illogical things. It made him unhappy in a different way.

"Why don't you stop Gran from telling the twins a lot of stuff that's not true?" I asked Dad after she'd caught the bus back to the city.

"Facing up to the truth is more difficult than people are capable of at certain times," he said.

"Well, she's having a terrible influence on those two," I said. "Tim's going to end up more of a nut-bar than he already is. Right now he's down in the garden seeing if he can feel Mum's presence."

Then I felt terrible when I saw Dad's face. He never went into the garden any more since Mum died.

"We have to be very patient with Gran just now," he said. "It's a dreadful thing to outlive your child. She'd like to come up more often. She thinks you children need her."

"Well, we don't," I said.

"Maybe she needs you."

"You won't let her come more often, will you?"

"I told her we'd be happy to see her whenever she can spare the time. I think it might help her to be with us, rather than grieving alone."

Oh, great, I thought. Just what I needed! So off I went again walking down to the marina.

That was my glorious summer! And it was supposed to be the best summer of my life, the one time I got to go away on holiday like a normal kid.

5

DAD SAID THE best thing we could do was to carry on with our daily routines and keep busy. That was so typical of him. Say one thing and do another. He didn't carry on with his daily routine. He'd taken a leave of absence from the university, and when he wasn't in the kitchen fixing a bowl of cornflakes, then changing his mind and leaving a soggy mess for somebody else to clear up, he sat in the living room staring into space.

Kelly insisted on coming in even though we didn't need her help with Mum any more, and she had her hands full with summer school. She planned to start a course to be a schoolteacher in the fall.

"I knew something terrible was going to happen," she said. "My horoscope said someone close to you will die. I said so to Jake."

She'd met Jake in an English class and she was hanging out with him all the time. He was really nice. When he came over with her, he changed the burned-out lightbulbs and took out the garbage that had piled up.

"And here I thought going to college would finally knock some sense into you and put an end to all that horoscope nonsense, Kelly," Dad said. "But perhaps that's too much to hope for."

"That man sure has a short fuse," Jake said. "Anyone talked to me like that I'd be out of here."

"It's just his way," Kelly said. "I take it as a compliment because he talks to me like I'm one of the family."

When Gran came, Dad went to his study and closed the door, but he didn't work on his computer. He just sat there looking at the empty screen. Gran sat at the dining-room table that was piled up with cards and envelopes. She was writing thank-you notes to all the neighbors who'd sent cards and letters. She tried to get me to help.

"Don't you even want to read the kind things they wrote?

"No," I said. "I didn't ask them to send cards. It's not like it's Christmas or somebody's birthday."

Dad had asked Gran to sort out Mum's things, but Gran said she couldn't bring herself to do that just yet. So Kelly got busy and started putting things in boxes to go to the Thrift store. I thought I'd never go into the Thrift store again, because I didn't want to see Mum's sweaters and blouses on coathangers there, and I didn't want to see people buying them.

Then Kelly asked me to come and help her decide what to do with the stuff in Mum's bedside table. So I went into Mum's room.

It gave me a creepy feeling. The vases were full of flowers because Tim and Toby were still bringing in fresh ones and changing the water, even though they weren't getting paid for it.

Kelly had put a lot of stuff in piles on the bed. There was a box of letters and cards that Dad had sent Mum before they were married. There were some boxes of jewelry and a lot of pretty silk scarves that Dad had given her for presents. We decided to take the jewelry down to the bank and put it in a safety deposit box. Kelly said maybe some of Mum's friends would like a scarf for a memento. I said I didn't want to give the scarves away. I didn't want to run into people in the supermarket wearing Mum's scarves.

I was just stuffing the scarves back in the bedside table when I saw something on top of the pretty paper that lined the bottom of the drawer. It was a big brown envelope.

It had my name on it in big letters. I sat on the bed and opened it.

Inside there were three typed letters. They were from a hospital and they were written to Dr. and Mrs. David Fremedon. The first one said that a baby was available. They were letters about my adoption.

The third letter wasn't typed. It was written in Mum's handwriting that had got very shaky in the past year. It wasn't a long letter and it began, "My dearest Ellen" and ended, "Love always, Mum."

"Ellen?" Kelly said.

"Yes?" I said, looking up.

"I've asked you twice. These letters from your dad? Do you think they should go into the safety deposit box with the jewelry?"

I just looked at her.

"Oh, honey," she said. "You've gone as white as a sheet. This is too hard on you. I shouldn't have bothered you with it. Your gran should be doing this. Let's stop for now, and I'll get us a bite to eat."

"I'm going outside," I said.

"That's right," she said. "Get a bit of fresh air. It'll make you feel better."

I picked up the envelope and went down to

Somecot. One of the drawers in my desk has a lock and key. I put the envelope in there, locked the drawer and put the key in the pocket of my jeans. Then I headed down the road to the beach. It was high tide so there was only a narrow strip of sand left, with no crabs on it. I walked along until I came to the big rock I like to sit on. I climbed on top of it, found a smooth patch with no barnacles and sat there looking out over the water.

Usually I calm down when I've been sitting on my rock for a while, but this time I didn't. My heart was beating *tick tock, tick tock* so hard I could practically feel it against my rib cage.

After about half an hour, I decided to go back and read Mum's letter.

I went down the garden to Somecot. Toby was sitting by himself on the path in Mum's cottage garden. We'd decided we were going to keep Mum's garden weeded and watered just the way she liked it. He was pulling out weeds from between the slates and putting them in a pail. Maybe he was trying to feel Mum's presence.

I went into Somecot, closed the door and locked it. Then I unlocked the desk drawer and took out the envelope. I sat down on the beanbag chair Jenny gave me for my last birthday and read Mum's letter. This is what it said:

My dearest Ellen,
One day you will want to find your birth mother. These letters will help you to find her. I'm sure she will be happy to meet you. I hope you will get to know each other and be good friends. Don't be afraid. A person can have many friends and brothers and sisters but only one mother, and I will always be your real mother. Nothing will ever change that. You've been a wonderful daughter.
Love always,
Mum

I didn't want to find my birth mother. Mum was my mother and I didn't want another one. I thought about how she always listened when I told her about Spotz. I asked her if you could meet a boy you liked at my age and then never meet anyone you liked as well for the whole rest of your life.

Mum thought very seriously for a while. Then she said it could happen but it didn't happen often, because life's very long and you meet a lot of different people along the way. She said that a lot of unexpected things happen. Then she told me about how she met Dad and they decided to get married, and I started to cheer up.

Then I thought about all the things I hadn't

done for her. How I sometimes forgot all about changing the water in the vases in her room. Sometimes I went in and all the flowers were dead and dried up, and after I threw them out I didn't put fresh ones in the vases for days. And I remembered the table outside her room that was empty the day I left for Toronto. The flowers had been in her room all night filling the air with carbon dioxide.

After a while, I put the letter back in the drawer and locked it. Then I went outside and walked back to the waterfront, where the tide was starting to turn.

6

I COULDN'T STOP thinking about the papers I'd found in Mum's drawer. I'd been born in a hospital called the Himalayan Cedar Clinic. The letter showed that Mum and Dad had gone to pick me up a week after I was born. I imagined the nurse handing me over to Dad. Then I thought it wouldn't be Dad who was carrying me. It would be Mum because she wasn't ill then. She was young, like in the pictures at the memorial service. And Dad had loads of hair when we started being a family. Maybe they put me in a baby buggy and wheeled me down the road.

Then I started thinking about the woman who was my birth mother. What did she do after she gave me away? Did she just leave the hospital and go home to her other kids and cook supper for them? Did they all live in a shack where there wasn't much food? Did she ever wonder what had happened to me?

It was all I could think about.

When I was staying with Dimsie, we watched a movie called *Great Expectations.* It was about a girl called Estella who got adopted by a rich but very nasty old woman. Estella was very proud because she was beautiful, but later she found out her real mother had murdered someone.

"What would you do if you were adopted and you found out your real mother was a murderer?" Dimsie said. She must have forgotten I was adopted.

"I'd go and visit her in prison."

"My dad says a lot of people get charged with murder and end up in prison when they're innocent all along," Dimsie said.

"Well, I'd try to find out who the real murderer was and get my mother out of prison," I said.

"I'd help you," Dimsie said. "We could look stuff up on the internet and find out who was really guilty."

After that we fell asleep, and I forgot all about the movie and Dimsie's question. Now I remembered it, and it scared me.

But I didn't want to talk to Dimsie. When she called I didn't go to the phone or call back, and when she sent messages I didn't reply.

It was Jenny I needed to talk to.

Jenny and I were always talking about my birth parents. As soon as I'd found out I was adopted, she'd put a bee in my bonnet about finding them.

"It's funny you don't want to know about them," she said, "because generally you're so nosy."

"Well, nobody's nosy about themselves," I said. "They're nosy about other people. I'll find out about my birth parents one day but I'm not in any hurry because Mum and Dad are my parents."

I often got mad at the way they treated me. They were hard on me, and they favored the twins just because they were younger and had been born the regular way. But I didn't really think any other parents would treat me better. After all, my birth parents gave me away as soon as I was born.

Sometimes, though, I did wonder about my birth mother, but I guess I was scared. Maybe she was a horrible person who wouldn't like me. Maybe she was beautiful and had a lot of other children. Maybe the other kids were all girls who were gorgeous and had long golden hair and wouldn't want me in the family because I wear glasses and my hair is dark and frizzy.

"That's not very likely," Jenny said. "We all look a bit like our parents."

"Maybe they'll all have glasses and frizzy hair and look like a freak show and I won't want to be part of that family," I said.

Then we got to laughing, and Jenny drew a whole family that looked exactly like me. She was doing a lot of cartoons at the time, and they were pretty funny. But later I wondered if I had other brothers and sisters and what they looked like. I tanned easily so maybe they were First Nations like Jake or born in a foreign country.

One time we asked Jenny's mum's partner Cathy, who's an RCMP officer, about tracing birth parents. Cathy said the adoption agencies had all the records, and I could apply to meet my birth mother when I was older. I was too young to do it now and the officials wouldn't let someone my age apply for the information. Mum and Dad would have to help me.

She said I'd want to do it later because I'd need to know if any health problems or diseases ran in my family.

How scary was that, I thought. A family that didn't want you, a mother who gave you away, and diseases you didn't know you had. So I put it out of my mind.

Now I was dwelling on it all the time, and my curiosity was getting the better of me. Mum said she hoped my birth mother and I would be friends and help each other out. So she must have known something about her. Dad must have known about her, too, but you couldn't ask him anything. All he did was pull stuff out of the fridge, then decide not to eat it and leave it attracting ants on the counter. And then when you asked him what to do with it, he got mad.

I lay in bed night after night wondering if my birth mother was very poor and lonely. Suppose she was ill like Mum and needed somebody to look after her?

I needed to talk to Jenny in the worst way, but she'd finally given up on me. She'd stopped creeping into Somecot while I was away and leaving things on my desk.

One day I fished all the stuff out of my wastebasket and put it on my desk. I opened all the cards and read the messages. She'd gone to a lot of trouble, and the cards were really nice. She'd stuck origami butterflies and doves and cranes on them. I arranged them in a row on my desk so that she'd see them if she came by. But she didn't come by any more. I couldn't really blame her.

Jenny and I got mad at each other all the time,

and we said a lot of things we didn't really mean. In the past, though, we'd always made up. But I'd never been as mean as I was that summer, even when she'd changed her ticket and flown right back from Saskatchewan in case I needed her. And she'd given up the art lessons that were the thing she cared most about and had been planning all year.

I didn't think we'd make up this time.

I hated doing errands because I kept running into people who asked me how we were doing, as if we'd all come down with chicken pox or something. I was avoiding all the neighbors. But sometimes Dad or Gran sent me down to the store for something we'd run out of. I walked very slowly past Jenny's house, hoping she'd see me and come running out. I looked out for her all over the village, but there was no sign of her in any of the usual places. I figured she'd either found a new best friend, or she was in her room all the time drawing and painting and trying to make up for the art classes she was missing. I knew that art school was expensive, and I wondered if she'd got her money back when she left.

I wondered what would happen when school started. For years I'd called at her house and we'd walked to school together. We sat side by side in class unless a teacher moved us for talking too much. We always ate lunch together and swapped sandwiches and stuff.

I remembered how lonely I'd been before Jenny came to live in Partridge Cove. Then I stopped being a loner and my whole life had changed. Now it had changed again. I'd lost my mother and I'd lost my best friend, and I was all by myself.

Off I went to the marina. I disturbed as many seals as I could, and then I walked along the beach where the baby crabs were washed up by the tide.

Then I sat on my rock and stared at the water.

7

A FEW NIGHTS later we'd just had supper and I was lying on my bed looking at a crack in the ceiling when the doorbell rang. Nobody answered it. That made me mad. I knew Dad was sitting in the living room doing nothing, and the twins were in their room not doing anything important. They all expected me to open the door and talk to whoever it was. Probably some neighbor who'd decided to bring leftovers from some rotten food they'd had for their own dinner. Then I'd have to say how grateful we were and tell them we were all doing fine. Then Gran would write them one of her stupid notes.

Eventually they'd probably just leave whatever they'd brought on the doorstep. When we didn't answer the door, people usually just left stuff on the step so we could trip over it the next time we went out. The day before I'd almost put my foot in a rhubarb pie. I hate rhubarb. But even more I hated everybody feeling sorry for us.

I wanted to put a big sign on the door saying NO FLOWERS NO PIES NO FOOD WE AREN'T HUNGRY JUST LEAVE US ALONE.

So I just lay there and let the bell ring again. Whoever it was couldn't take a hint.

Then I got to thinking maybe it was Jenny, who was giving me one final chance to be friends again. She'd know we were all home and when nobody came to the door, she'd go away and never ever come back.

The doorbell rang again. It sounded like whoever it was had got their finger stuck on the bell.

I finally ran upstairs and opened the door.

It wasn't Jenny. It was Higg.

I didn't feel like talking to him. For one thing, I didn't want anybody else asking how we were doing.

"Hi!" I said. At least he wasn't carrying a bunch of flowers or leftovers from his dinner.

"Is your dad home, Ellen?" he said.

By then Dad had finally got it together and dragged himself out of the living room.

"Good evening, Brian," he said.

"Can I come in for a moment?" Higg said.

"Sure," Dad said.

They went into the living room. Dad asked Higg if he could offer him something, but he said it so halfheartedly that I didn't blame Higg for saying no thanks.

"This is business, sort of," he said. "Ellen, you can stay if you want."

I didn't really want to, but I sat down anyway.

"It's about the marina," Higg said. "A big developer wants to take it over and improve it."

"Oh, really?" Dad said.

He was leaning forward and studying his shoes. I don't know if he even heard what Higg was saying.

"It needs fixing up," I said, just for something to say. "The holes in the ramps are so big in places a person could fall through them and drown."

"That's only part of it," Higg said. "He plans to build a series of six-story condominiums, a high-rise apartment building, a hotel and a restaurant all along the waterfront. There'll be huge parking garages. Underground."

"Well, that's a lot of nonsense," Dad said. "Underground parking garages! They'll get flooded. Besides, the whole area is zoned for single-family dwellings, and the waterfront is zoned for public use."

"He's applied to have it rezoned," Higg said.

"He can apply all he wants," Dad said, "but the application won't pass. Nobody wants to see a series of high-rise concrete buildings all along the Partridge Cove waterfront."

"Oh, yes they do," Higg said. "Many of the local merchants say it would bring in more business. The builders and contractors and real estate agents say it will create jobs. A lot of older people who can't keep up their houses say they'd like to live in waterfront apartments. They've got it into their heads it'll be affordable housing, when in fact it will be luxury condos for millionaires. Boaters want a better marina. The developer has put out brochures showing how beautiful the new marina and the buildings will be. There are petitions on the counters in all the stores. They're filling up with the signatures of people in favor of the new development."

"Is that so?" Dad said. He didn't sound very interested.

"The increased traffic around here will make the place impossible for pedestrians," Higg said, "not to mention problems with sewage and water. If this goes through it will be the end of Partridge Cove as we know it."

"I suppose it will," Dad said.

"We have to put a stop to it before it goes any further," Higg said. "We have to organize a group of people who are willing to fight this developer."

"I shouldn't think you'd have time with your teaching and coaching the debaters, and looking after a young child."

Higg's a single parent because his wife left him last year, and his kid, Thumper, is only two.

"Someone has to do it," Higg said. "I hope we can count on your help."

Dad didn't say anything.

"At least you'll attend the meetings, won't you?" Higg said.

"I'm not sure," Dad said. "Lots to do around here these days."

"Well, I've brought these brochures for you to look at."

He put them on the coffee table.

"Thanks," Dad said, but he didn't look at them.

"Well, I'd better be getting back to Thumper," Higg said after a while.

"You left him all by himself?" I said.

"Of course not. Kelly and Jake stopped by, and they offered to look after him while I came over here."

Dad got up to see him out.

"By the way, Ellen," Higg said as he was leaving. "Jenny's back home now. She was over in Vancouver visiting her dad all last week. I saw her at the school today and I think she has some things she'd like to talk over with you."

"She would?" I said. "Did she say that?"

"She'd like to see you so why not give her a call or go over in the morning," he said.

When I went back to my room I felt better than I had in a long time.

8

SOMETIMES I WISHED I lived in a city where nobody knows anybody else and you hardly ever bump into anybody you know. The next morning we ran out of bread, so Dad told me to go down to the village to pick up a loaf. I was just walking out of the store when someone called my name.

It was Mrs. Banks. She was standing chatting with Mrs. Fenwick. So I had to go back and talk to them.

"I'm very pleased to hear you're all doing so well," Mrs. Fenwick said, after I told them Dad was fine, the twins were fine, Gran was fine, and I was fine.

"You've been going through a difficult time, a very difficult time," Mrs. Banks said.

Tell me about it, I wanted to say, but I bit my tongue.

"I hope you haven't gone off your food," Mrs. Fenwick said. "You have to keep your strength up, you know. That's what I always tell my friends who've lost a loved one."

"I couldn't face my food for days after Rover died," Mrs. Banks said.

"I was just taking these pots of jam over to the food bank," Mrs. Fenwick said. "Why don't you take one? It's my homemade blackberry."

"And take a jar of this applesauce," Mrs. Banks said.

Finally I got away from them and headed home, loaded down with jars.

I was just passing Jenny's house, when the jars got so heavy I couldn't go any farther, and my legs seemed to carry me up the path to her door.

I'd already rung the bell when I remembered how rude I'd been when Anne and Cathy drove me home from the airport. But it was too late to run away because the door opened and Anne was there in front of me.

"Why, Ellen," she said. "How good to see you! Come in! Jenny's in her room. She'll be thrilled to see you."

I put the bread and jam and applesauce on the kitchen table and went to Jenny's room. The door was ajar so I pushed it open and stood in the doorway without saying anything.

Jenny was sitting in a chair. She was concentrating so hard on a sketchpad on her lap that she didn't see me.

"Hi!" I said after a while.

"Ellen!" she said. She grinned like she was actually glad to see me.

"I heard you went to Vancouver."

"I stayed with my dad and Sally."

"How did it go?"

"Like always," she said, making a face. "I mostly babysat my little brother, but I did get to go to the art gallery."

I felt bad when she said that. I wondered if it made up for missing so much of her art course.

"Guess who I saw?" she said.

I didn't say anything.

"Spotz. He was at the art gallery with two girls."

"Oh!" I hadn't been thinking too much about Spotz lately.

"Are you still sad because he had to move?" Jenny said. Then she looked embarrassed. I guess she remembered I had a lot more to be sad about.

"Did he ask about me?" I said.

"Well, we weren't talking very long," she said. So I knew he hadn't.

Jenny had pictures of her dad and her little brother on the wall. They were photos that she'd had enlarged and put in beautiful frames.

I went over and looked at them.

"I could show you how to make one like that from a picture of your mother," she said. "Would you like that?"

"Yes," I said. "I really would."

I thought about the package of papers I'd found, and how I'd wanted to talk to Jenny about my adoption. But now I didn't know how to start.

"I wanted to tell you something..." I said. Then I thought about Mum's letter to me and I got a lump in my throat. I couldn't go on.

"Oh, Ellen, that's okay," Jenny said. "You don't have to say sorry. I knew how rotten you were feeling. Don't feel bad. I was getting fed up with the art school anyway."

"You were? Why?"

"Well, it wasn't the art, it was the bagpipers. They were having a bagpipe clinic at the same time. One bagpipe's bad enough, but can you imagine a whole squad of them, blowing and squeezing those things, and playing the same tune over and over again? Even when they stopped, I could still hear the tune in my head. They sounded like a rooster that's trying to crow while somebody's strangling it."

I laughed.

"Gran says the queen gets wakened up every morning by a bagpiper playing under her window."

"No wonder she always looks grumpy," Jenny said.

"Higg said you wanted to talk to me about something."

"He did?" She looked puzzled. "I don't remember telling him that, but I guess we should be getting our school stuff rounded up."

So we decided to get together after lunch. I was going to pick out my favorite photo of Mum, and we were going to make lists of what we needed for school.

On the way out of the house I picked up my packages.

"People are treating us like we're the food bank," I said. Then I remembered that Anne had sent over a pie. "It's really nice of them."

"Well, here's a batch of corn muffins just out of the oven," Anne said. "They aren't sweet so if you like them sweeter, put some syrup on them. Let me give you this bottle of maple syrup to go with them."

I really had my arms full then, so Jenny walked home with me and carried some of the stuff.

For lunch Dad and I had the corn muffins with

syrup on them, and the twins had some toast with Mrs. Fenwick's jam on it. We had applesauce for dessert. It wasn't much of a lunch. The twins were pretty quiet.

"Dad," I said, "you know the developer Higg told you about, the one that wants to put a row of high-rises along the waterfront?"

"Yes," Dad said. "I believe he left some brochures. They're around here somewhere, if Kelly hasn't thrown them out."

He poured some more maple syrup on a muffin. Then he changed his mind about eating it and pushed his plate away.

"Well, there's a big tent outside the store," I said. "The developer's hired a lot of students. They're talking to all the people who go in to buy groceries. They're asking them to sign petitions in favor of the development. They've got hundreds of signatures already because everybody's signing. You get a free pen if you sign."

"I'll go and sign up," Tim said. "We need pens for school."

"Do they give you a new one every time?" Toby said. "We could sign this afternoon and again tomorrow."

"We could sign Dad's name," Tim said, "I'm really good at faking his — "

"Don't you dare sign those petitions!" Dad said. "If I catch you anywhere near them, I'll box your ears."

Then he got up from the table, went into his study and banged the door.

Boy, our family was really falling apart. I'd never heard Dad shout at the twins before.

"I wish I was dead and in a better place with Mum," Tim said. "We never get to do anything." He wiped his eyes on his sleeve.

In the end, Dad came out and gave the twins ten dollars each to buy school supplies. He said he'd walk down to the village himself after lunch and look into what was going on.

9

IT WAS A FEW days later before I finally got up my nerve to tell Jenny. We were walking along the beach.

"You know how you always said I should find my birth mother?"

"Sure."

"Well, since Mum died I've found out a lot of information. I think I can find her."

"You want to do it *now*?" She sounded shocked.

"I was born in a hospital in a place called Burnaby."

"That's just outside Vancouver."

"You know where it is?"

"Well, I've driven through it with my dad. There's a big university on a mountain. Simon Fraser."

So my mother might have been a student like Kelly, maybe studying to be a teacher or something. Or maybe she was a foreign student who was all alone with a family on the other side of the world.

"The hospital's called the Himalayan Cedar Clinic," I said.

"That's a funny name," Jenny said. "It doesn't even sound Canadian. The Himalayas are mountains in India."

"Maybe it's a hospital for Indian people," I said. "Maybe my mother was from India."

I suddenly had a picture in my mind of a beautiful dark-haired woman in a sari, like the ones in *National Geographic.*

Then I told Jenny about the envelope and the letters to Mum and Dad from the woman who ran the hospital.

"I could ask my dad about that hospital," Jenny said.

Things happened quite fast after that. Jenny's dad's a doctor in Vancouver and she said she'd call him that night and ask him about the Himalayan Cedar place. But it was two days before she managed to talk to him because her stepmother doesn't like Jenny much, and she doesn't pass on her messages.

Her dad said he knew the place very well because he used to drive past it all the time. It was a small clinic for private patients and not a regular hospital. It closed down about ten years ago and he didn't have a clue about the records. They could have been destroyed when the place closed down.

"It looks like I'll never find my birth mother after all," I said.

But two days later Jenny phoned and said she'd thought of something.

"What about the people who worked at the hospital?" she said. "There must have been doctors and nurses, and some of them must still be around. Ten years isn't a very long time."

That made me think about the name on the letter the hospital had sent to my parents about picking me up. I decided to show Jenny all the letters except the one that Mum had written me. So we went down to Somecot and she read them.

"That's not a very usual name," Jenny said. "We can look it up on the computer."

The name was Ivy Roscoe-Jones.

"Dad won't let me use the computer. I can't even go into his study these days. He's always in there with the door shut. If you knock on the door, he tells you to go away because he's busy."

"Well, we can look it up at the library."

I didn't feel like going to the library and talking to the librarians just then, so Jenny said she'd do it for me. There were three listings under that name but none of them had the right initial. Jenny said that was okay because a lot of women just put their husbands' names in the phone book. So we decided to call the three Roscoe-Joneses. We went to her house when Anne and Cathy were out.

The first one Jenny called had an answering machine. The names were Don and Marge.

I called the next one and a woman answered. When I asked to speak to Ivy Roscoe-Jones, she said that was her mother-in-law and she didn't live there.

"Could you tell us where she lives and give us her phone number?"

The woman said her mother-in-law lived in Victoria, but she didn't like to give out her number without asking permission. She'd be talking to her in a few days and she'd ask if it was all right.

"Could you give me your name and tell me why you want to talk to her?" she said.

That made me so nervous, I just hung up.

After we recovered from that, Jenny said she'd see if she was in the Victoria phone book. Jenny was thinking a lot more clearly about all this than I was.

There was only one Roscoe-Jones in the Victoria phone book, and her initials were V.I.

"I bet that's her," she said. "Let's call her."

"I don't know."

"Are you getting cold feet?"

"What will we say?" I was scared but I felt bad saying I didn't want to go through with it after Jenny had made a zillion phone calls, long distance. "I bet she won't tell me anything anyway. Like everyone says, you have to be older and there's a lot of red tape."

"You could get your dad to help."

"I told you I can't talk to Dad about anything these days. He gets mad and starts yelling, and then he goes in his study and slams the door."

"Your dad yells at you?"

"At the twins, mainly. But he got mad at Kelly when she asked him a simple question about Mum's jewelry. Besides, I don't want to talk to him about this."

The only thing anybody could talk to my dad about these days was something that didn't involve our family, like the marina. After I told him about the tent outside the supermarket, he'd taken a walk and looked into it.

He'd hardly gone out of the house since Mum died so I was glad he was going for a walk. When he came back he was in a temper. He'd been in one of the stores in the village and seen a petition on the counter. After that, he checked out the other stores in the village, and discovered they were all collecting signatures. He said he tried to warn Mr. Floyd in the Clothes Loft that Partridge Cove was going to end up like Monte Carlo. There'd be casinos and rich tourists speeding around in flashy cars and a lot of restaurants that were too expensive for normal people to eat in.

"You've made a good point there," Mr. Floyd told him. "We could use a casino. I'll suggest it to the developer. It could put this place on the map."

"It could put us on the map all right," Dad said, after he'd stomped in the door. "Especially if we lose our water, destroy the inlet and end up with a row of leaky condos. It's the most outrageous thing I've ever heard of. Most of the people signing these petitions are not from Partridge Cove at all. They're from all the neighboring towns. Some are from Victoria."

He was still fuming about it at supper. We were having waffles, the frozen kind that you put in the toaster. Kelly had come by with some blackberries she and Jake had picked. She whipped up some cream to put on top of the waffles and that made them pretty yummy.

"I called Brian the minute I got home. I told him I wanted to join the group that's fighting to preserve the waterfront and the rural character of Partridge Cove."

"What did he say?"

"Well, that's the odd thing. He said there wasn't a group at the moment but there was a lot of interest in forming one. Didn't you understand, Ellen, that he said there was a group when he warned us about the development the other night?"

I was just going to say yes, when I caught Kelly's eye. She winked at me, so I said I didn't remember.

"Now Brian says he's all caught up in the start of school and getting Thumper into daycare and organizing the debating society. He asked me if I'd send out some emails and get a handful of people together in The Creamery one evening next week."

"That's a good idea," Kelly said. "Jake and me'll be there. I'll get my mom to come with us."

"I'll tell Anne and Cathy," I said. "I bet they'll want to come. And Mr. and Mrs. Banks, too."

"Well, I suppose I'd better get on with it, then," Dad said, and he headed into his study.

"Your dad'll perk up, Ellen," Kelly whispered to me, "now that he's got a fight on his hands. You'll see. It's just what he needs. He'll be back to his old self in no time."

"That'll be a relief," I said.

10

My meeting with Mrs. Roscoe-Jones turned out better than I expected.

What happened was that Dad decided he was going to drive down to the city to see if he could find some of the Partridge Cove records at the courthouse. He said if any of us kids wanted to come along we could. Of course, we all did. He'd drop us off and we could all meet for lunch in the cafeteria at The Bay at noon. The twins wanted to spend the morning in the bug zoo. I said I was going to look for a new pair of jeans.

It wasn't as hard as we thought to get Mrs. Roscoe-Jones to agree to see me. Jenny came up with another brilliant idea. I called her and said I was doing a report, and that I wanted to talk to her about an old building in Burnaby that I thought she knew something about: the Himalayan Cedar Clinic.

"Why, I was the administrator there some years ago, right until the time it closed," she said. "I also knew the house before it became a clinic. I'd love to talk to you about it. I have some pictures, too."

Jenny was really terrific about all this.

"Why are you all dressed up just to buy jeans?" the twins asked when we were getting into the car. I was wearing a blouse and a jacket that Jenny had lent me because she didn't think blue jeans and a T-shirt would make the right impression.

"This is what people wear in the city," I said. "They don't go around in old beat-up pants and stupid T-shirts with SAVE OUR PLANET on them."

After Dad dropped us off I found a flower shop and bought a bouquet of flowers. This was Jenny's idea, too. She said it would be hard for Ivy to refuse to help me when I'd given her an expensive bunch of flowers.

The flowers I picked out were nice enough, though I couldn't believe how little you got for twenty dollars. I could have got better ones from our garden, except Dad would have wondered why I was taking a bouquet of flowers to the city.

"Is it for your mom?" the girl in the shop asked

while she was wrapping the flowers in paper. I was so shocked by the question that I got a lump in my throat, and I couldn't breathe. She stopped what she was doing and stared at me.

"My mum died," I said as soon as I got my voice back. "The flowers are for somebody else."

"Oh, you poor thing. Was it an accident?"

"No. She was ill for a long time."

"Well, let me make this bouquet really special."

She added a lot more flowers, wrapped them in cellophane and tied a piece of colored straw around it. By the time she finished, the bouquet was enormous. It looked super and it smelled terrific, too.

It didn't take me long to find the address that Mrs. Roscoe-Jones had given me over the phone. It was an apartment building on the road that runs by the water. I took the elevator to the third floor and knocked on the door.

"What beautiful flowers!" she said when she saw me. "How did you know stargazer lilies are my favorite?"

She took ages arranging them in a vase before she got around to asking me how she could help me. She had some pictures of the Himalayan Cedar Clinic spread out on the coffee table in front of the couch. I felt a bit guilty when I saw them.

"I was born in that clinic," I said.

"Were you?" she said. "Then that explains your interest. It was a very beautiful place. The grounds were lovely, with some remarkable tree plantings. There were trees from all over the world. You can see the Himalayan cedars in the pictures. The original owner was a world traveler, and his wife was a botanist. That explains the name of the clinic."

"It does?" I said. "I thought maybe it was a clinic for people from India."

"Oh, no. It was a private clinic for local people in the Vancouver area, though people came from all parts of the United States. It was an expensive place."

"I was adopted," I said. "And I'd like to know something about my birth mother."

It came out all in a burst, not like I'd planned, but I wanted to stop her from talking about the clinic.

"Goodness!" she said.

"That's why I came to you," I said. "For help."

"My dear, such matters are highly confidential. One must go through channels. And you are so young. Is there any reason why at this time…?"

"My mother died," I said. "The one who adopted me…"

The minute I said that the lump came back in

my throat. I tried to swallow it down, but it wouldn't go away and I couldn't go on.

"Oh, my dear, I'm so sorry," she said. "Was this recently?"

I nodded.

She handed me a box of tissues and then she got up and brought me a glass of water. Then she offered me a chocolate out of a little gold box. She didn't seem to know what to do next.

After I'd got back on track, I told her how old I was and where I lived and what Dad did. She wanted to know all about my family. For a long time she didn't say anything, and I wondered if she was trying to remember all the babies who were adopted.

"I guess you can't remember every baby that was adopted?" I said.

She didn't answer my question.

"How did you find me?" she asked.

I told her about the letters in the envelope, and how I'd looked up her name in the phone books.

"I do remember, my dear," she said at last. "It was a very unusual case. I worried about it at the time. Not that I did anything illegal. I wouldn't do that. But it was rather irregular. A counselor at the university got in touch with me."

"Why was it unusual? Was there something

wrong with my birth mother? Was she a student from a foreign country?"

"No. It was not unusual in that sense. It was an unusual arrangement, which at the time seemed perfectly feasible, but I always wondered... In some ways it was very usual...a young girl in distress, and a faculty member who had a colleague looking for just such a child. But one never knows..."

"Can you tell me about my birth mother?"

"My dear, I couldn't do that even if I wanted to. These are very complicated matters. But I will do something."

I waited while the clock on the mantelpiece ticked and the stargazer lilies smelled very strong.

"I cannot speak to her directly. I am not able to do that. But I will get a message to her and tell her that you would like to contact her. Then it must be up to her. If she wishes to see you, she will. If, for some reason, she doesn't, then you must respect her wishes."

"I just want to know who I am," I said. "So I'd like to know who she is." Actually, I hadn't thought much about meeting her. Mostly I wanted to know what she was like.

"I want you to promise me one thing," she said. "Will you promise me something?"

"It depends."

"I want very much for you to tell your father about this. Will you do that?"

"Okay," I said, though I didn't want to. But at least she hadn't set a time. I didn't have to tell him right away.

I was in Mrs. Roscoe-Jones's apartment for such a long time that Dad and the twins had almost finished their lunch by the time I got up to the third floor of The Bay.

"Really, Ellen!" Dad said.

"I lost track of the time," I said. "Don't worry. I'm not hungry."

But Dad insisted I get something to eat. He said if we had a big lunch now, he wouldn't need to cook anything for supper. Not that he was cooking much for supper anyway these days.

So I went and got pasta with prawns and mushrooms in it, and a roll on the side.

"We could have stayed longer in the bug zoo," Tim said. "But Dad came and dragged us out so we wouldn't keep you waiting."

"And we just missed seeing a praying mantis eat its mate," Toby said. "If we go back after lunch it will be too late."

"Well, you aren't going back after lunch so you can forget that," Dad said.

"It starts off by biting off the mate's head," Tim said.

"And they go on mating even after the mate doesn't have any head," Toby said.

"The mate makes eggs that are all frothy," Tim said.

My appetite came back after a while, so I had lemon meringue pie and ice cream for dessert. And the twins nagged Dad to let them have second desserts to keep me company.

The trip home was a nightmare. The twins were completely hyped up on their visit to the bug zoo. They said they were thinking of starting one of their own. I could see that bugs were all we'd be hearing about from now on.

"You can get a tarantula for forty bucks," Tim said. "And that includes the cage. They're a lot cheaper here. I wish we lived in the city."

"You don't have forty bucks," I said.

"If we could borrow it and buy a tarantula, we could charge a dollar for kids to come and see it. Then we could pay the money back."

"Nobody's going to pay a dollar just to see a big hairy spider," I said.

"They would if they could watch it eating live crickets," Toby said.

"Yuck," I said.

"We are not having a tarantula in the house," Dad said, as he swerved to dodge a cyclist that pulled out in front of us without warning.

"But everybody except us has a pet," Toby said. Sean Floyd has a dog and a rabbit. Wyatt's got a dog called Roxy, and Jordan's got two cats and a gerbil."

"If I hear one more word about spiders, or dogs, or gerbils, I'm pulling over and leaving the two of you on the side of the highway!"

Suddenly, a thought struck me.

The twins were back to being their usual obnoxious selves for the first time since Mum died.

It didn't make sense, but in a funny way, I was glad.

11

WE SOON FOUND out that it would be a long time before we heard the last of tarantulas. The twins came home the next week with the news that their teacher thought it would be great to have a tarantula in the classroom.

"It's going to be a class project," Toby said. "We've already started collecting crickets to feed it. I've got two in a jar."

"Oh, yeah? And how are you going to get the money to pay for it?" I said.

"We're having a bottle drive," Tim said. "We'll get the money from the deposits on empty bottles. All the kids are going to collect them."

"It'll take you all year to collect enough bottles to raise forty dollars," I said.

"No, it won't." Toby said. "We're having a competition. The kid that brings in the most bottles gets to name the tarantula."

"I'm going to get the most bottles and name it Amaryllis because that was Mum's favorite flower," Tim said. "I gave her one for Christmas last year and she said it made her happy every time she looked at it."

"She just said that because she didn't want to hurt your feelings," I said. "She didn't like waxy hot-house flowers. She liked garden flowers and wildflowers."

Things were getting back to normal around our house. It was true what Kelly said about Dad being his old self when he had a fight on his hands. He wasn't exactly cheerful, and it didn't take much to make him mad, like when Tim emptied all the pop and spring water bottles in the fridge so he could get the deposit on the empties. But at least he didn't just sit in the living room staring into space any more.

Mostly he was at his computer looking up information about the new development or on the phone discussing it with people. Although most of the storekeepers were still in favor of the development, all the neighbors objected to it once Dad explained it to them.

Mr. and Mrs. Banks and Mrs. Fenwick said they'd signed the petition because the young people who asked them to were so polite and clean-cut that it was a pleasure to talk to them. They thought it was a good thing to see students earning money for their college fees, and they hadn't paid much attention to what they were signing.

So in a way it was like old times, with Dad always busy in his study when I wanted to ask him something. Every so often I remembered that I'd promised Mrs. Roscoe-Jones that I would tell him about searching for my birth mother, but I always put it off until the next day, and then the next one after that.

"Have you told your dad yet?" Jenny asked me at least once a day.

"No," I'd say. "He's busy today. I'm going to tell him tomorrow."

In the end it was Dad himself who brought it up. He came out of his study one day when I was trying to scrape the guck off all the dishes that had piled up in the kitchen sink.

"Ellen," he said, "can you explain what this is about?"

He'd got a letter from a lawyer's office in Vancouver saying that if Miss Fremedon wished to pursue the matter she had discussed with Mrs.

Roscoe-Jones on a certain date, she should call the lawyer's office and make an appointment.

"Is this some mistake?" he said. "Who on earth is Mrs. Roscoe-Jones? And this date? It's the day we all went down to Victoria. Do you know anything about this?"

"Yes," I said.

"Well, would you kindly enlighten me?"

I told Dad about how I'd found the package in Mum's bedside table, how Jenny had made the phone calls, and how I'd visited Mrs. Roscoe-Jones and promised her I'd tell him about my search. The only thing I didn't tell him about was Mum's letter.

"And why didn't you tell me?"

"I was going to, but you were always busy with the marina stuff," I said.

"Well, I wish you'd spoken to me about all this before it got so far."

"You didn't want to hear about anything," I said. "You didn't want to hear about sorting out Mum's clothes. You didn't want to hear about the garden. You didn't want to hear about the people who sent cards, you didn't want to hear — "

"All right, all right," Dad said, holding up his hand. "I suppose I'm very much at fault as usual in this matter. Well, we must see what can be done. I suppose this lawyer represents...the person you want to get in touch with. I'll call the office and see if I can talk to him. And not a word about any of this to Gran or the twins."

As if.

Later Dad told me that he hadn't managed to get through to the lawyer. He'd only spoken to a secretary and he'd more or less been forced to make an appointment.

"So we'll have to go off to Vancouver," he said. "These lawyers are very annoying. They don't want to talk on the phone because I suppose it cuts into their billable hours. By the way, this lawyer is a 'she' not a 'he.'"

"What's billable hours?" I said.

"They demand a hefty fee of about two hundred dollars per hour, and they charge for every minute and probably every second they spend with you."

It wasn't possible to keep the trip to Vancouver a secret, of course.

"You seem to be spending a lot of time on this marina project, David," Gran said on her Sunday visit. "I hope it's yielding some results."

"It is time-consuming," Dad said, "but it will be worth all the effort if we manage to prevent the Partridge Cove waterfront from being ruined. By the way, I'm planning to slip over to Vancouver next week to consult with someone. I'll take Ellen along with me."

"What about school?" Gran said.

"She can take a day off without missing much," Dad said.

"That's not what you said when I wanted to take a day off to collect bottles," Tim said. "It's not fair."

"You know," Gran said. "I believe I'll come with you. I was thinking of going over to the mainland to find a replacement for that Wedgwood plate that Ellen broke when she helped me with the dishes last year. I haven't been able find the right match for my dinner service in Victoria."

"I was counting on you to be here to look after the twins," Dad said.

"We don't need looking after," Toby said. "Kelly and Jake can come after school and fix us something to eat."

"I don't like to depend on them," Dad said. "They're both busy with their courses. Someone needs to be here, though. Just in case the ferry is delayed."

"Remember the one that sank last year?" I said. "You'd better stay here, Gran, in case there's a ferry disaster and we never— "

"I'm not anticipating a ferry disaster," Dad said. "But I would feel more easy in my mind if a mature person were here when we're away. We do depend on you a great deal these days, Mother. I don't know what we'd do without you."

"Well, of course, if I'm really needed..." Gran said. "I suppose I could call ahead to the store, get them to set aside the plate and you could pick it up for me."

"I'd be happy to do that," Dad said, looking relieved.

"So would I," I said. "I'll make sure he doesn't forget."

And we smiled at each other.

12

DAD AND I drove straight to the law office from the ferry because we were afraid of being late for our appointment. It was in one of the tallest skyscrapers I'd ever seen. It was all steel and glass and there were about a million elevators taking people up and down.

We went up to the twenty-first floor. Once we got there, we sat in a waiting room for about fifteen minutes. Across the hall several secretaries were typing away with earphones on their heads.

After a while one of them got up and led us to a room where a woman was sitting at a big desk with two chairs facing it. She looked angry, as if we'd interrupted her in the middle of some important work. She just pointed to the chairs and didn't look up.

We sat down and I looked around the office. There were lots of bookshelves but the books on them all looked very heavy and boring. On the shelf behind the desk there was a photograph of an old man with a long beard and a black hat on his head.

Then I looked at the lawyer. Suddenly, I knew I'd seen her before. She was the hotshot lawyer who'd judged the public-speaking contest in Vancouver and chewed me out for not dressing up. She'd looked pretty messy herself, and Higg had said that was because she'd been sitting up all night in an airplane. But her hair was still sticking out all over the place, and she looked pale and tired. Maybe she was always flying through the night on airplanes.

"I'm not sure what you expect of me," she said.

"Excuse me?" Dad said.

I remembered what Dad had told me about billable hours, and I wondered if lawyers dragged out conversations like this on purpose so they could make more money. I hoped this meeting wouldn't cost Dad hundreds and hundreds of dollars.

"I'm not sure what you expect of me," she said again.

"I don't understand," Dad said. "We were instructed to make an appointment here."

"Exactly," she said. She spoke to Dad and ignored me completely. "I believe you are seeking information about the birth mother of your adopted daughter."

"That is quite correct," Dad said. "If you have any information about that person or any communication from her, we would be pleased to have it. We were hoping that she might be willing at some future time to meet with us, if that could be arranged."

There was another long silence. If this was costing over two hundred dollars an hour, I thought, we'd already spent fifty.

"You really don't understand, do you?" the lawyer said.

"I'm sorry?" Dad said.

The lawyer didn't say anything for what I figured was another ten dollars' worth of time. Then she spoke in quite a soft voice.

"I am she," she said.

We all stared at each other. At least, Dad and I stared at her. She looked down at her desk for another few minutes. Then she looked at Dad, avoiding me again as if she didn't want to know me.

After a while she went on in her normal voice.

"When the adoption was arranged over twelve years ago, I waived all rights and responsibilities.

The arrangement was a formal one but not a legal one. That was an error of judgment on my part, which I now deeply regret. I was young and inexperienced and received very bad advice from those who counseled me. However, at the time I believed the arrangement to be legally binding. I expected that to be the end of the matter and I moved on with my life. I put behind me what was a very unfortunate and rather sordid episode — "

"Madam," Dad said quite suddenly and loudly, as if he had just woken up. "I don't think my daughter needs to hear this. Ellen, wait outside."

He stood up, opened the door, pushed me outside and shut it behind me with a loud bang.

I felt as if I'd done something wrong. I sat in the waiting room in a state of shock. I thought I should never have opened that package in Mum's bedside table. I should never have gone to see Mrs. Roscoe-Jones.

Maybe I should never have been born.

Suddenly I heard Dad's voice very loud and angry through the closed door. You could hear him down the corridor, though I couldn't make out what he was saying. The secretary who'd showed us into the office smiled at me a bit nervously.

A man came in with a handful of papers and handed them to the secretary.

"What's the terror threat level today?" he said, nodding in the direction of the closed door.

"Orange," she said with a laugh that wasn't really a laugh.

"Oh, boy!" he said.

Then Dad's voice started up again. The man raised his eyebrows and looked at me and then at the secretary.

"A child custody case?" he said. "That's unusual for her, isn't it?"

"I'm not in the know on this one," the secretary said. "It seems to be highly confidential."

It seemed like ages before anything else happened. Dad's voice died down, and things went quiet for a long time. Then the door opened and Dad and the lawyer came out.

"We're going into the boardroom," the lawyer said to the secretary. "Have some coffee sent in."

We followed her down a long corridor into a room with more shelves of boring leather books along the walls. But this room had nice furniture and plants and a huge dining-room table in the middle. There was a group of armchairs in front of the window at one end and we sat in them.

A woman brought in a tray with a coffee pot on it, some bottles of juice, and a plate of muffins and shortbread cookies. Nobody said anything while she poured the coffee and handed out the cups. She gave me a glass of juice. It was cranberry, which I don't really like, but I drank a bit just to be polite.

"Ellen," the lawyer said, "my name is Sarah Maslin. I am your birth mother."

She looked at Dad as if she was checking to see that she'd got it right.

I didn't know what to say, so I told her I knew who she was because I'd seen her at the debating tournament the year before.

"I won a trophy in the public-speaking contest," I said. "In the novice category."

She didn't seem interested.

"If you have any questions you would like to ask me," she said. "I will try to answer them."

"Do I have any half-brothers and sisters?" I said.

"I never married," she said, "so there are no brothers and sisters."

"Are there any diseases I might come down with?" I said.

She and Dad both looked shocked. I don't know why I said that. It was hard to think straight.

"There are no hereditary diseases in my family that I am aware of," she said.

"Do I have any grandparents?" I said.

She reached for the cup of coffee she'd set on the table. She put another cube of sugar in it and then set it back down. She looked as if I'd asked something really difficult and she needed time to think about it.

"My mother is alive, so I suppose the answer is yes, you do have a grandmother," she said. She seemed so freaked out by that question that I couldn't think what to say next.

"What should I call you?" I said.

Again, she looked shocked.

"Sarah. Just call me Sarah."

"Will I see you again?"

"If you have any more questions, I will try to answer them for you. This could be done by telephone." She looked at Dad. "If a meeting is necessary I…it could be arranged."

"Perhaps this is enough for one day," Dad said. "We should let you get back to work." He sounded really tired.

"Thank you for bringing your daughter to see me," she said to Dad, and then they shook hands.

"Dad," I said when we got off the elevator, "we were in there for nearly two hours. That's five hundred dollars."

"We won't be charged," Dad said.

"What does 'sordid' mean?" I said.

He didn't answer and I thought I'd look it up when I got home.

"Did you like her?" I said.

He didn't answer that, either, so I asked him again, even though I knew the answer.

"We don't know her," he said after a while. "First impressions are often misleading."

But it wasn't my first impression, it was my second. My first impression had been very bad. My second impression was even worse.

I wished I'd never bothered to find my birth mother.

On the ferry we went into the Pacific Buffet in the front of the boat. It was quieter than the cafeteria and a lot more expensive, but Dad said we owed it to ourselves because we'd had a rough morning.

It was nice sitting at a table by the window looking out over the water. There were a lot of different dishes to choose from in the buffet and I had a bit of everything. Dad had a beer and didn't eat much. I ate every single thing on my plate.

I was just looking down at my empty plate and wondering if I should go back for seconds, when I remembered something.

"Dad," I said, "we forgot to pick up Gran's plate."

"Oh, my God," he said.

When I got home I went down to Somecot and locked the door. I sat at my desk and I wrote a letter.

Dear Mum,
I met my birth mother and I don't like her and Dad doesn't like her either so I don't think we will be friends like you said. I'm really really glad you adopted me and I'm glad you were my mum because I would have had a terrible life with her. She's called Sarah Maslin and she was the judge when I won my trophy. I told you about her and you said maybe her bark was worse than her bite. Well, it isn't. She is not a nice person, and nobody likes her. I don't want to see her any more. Thank you again for adopting me.
Love,
Ellen

Then I folded the letter up and put it in the drawer with Mum's letter to me and locked it.

13

I WAS GLAD Jenny was away the day after Dad and I went to Vancouver. When you've had a big disappointment, sometimes you don't want to talk about it for a while, even to your best friend. The day after that I went over to her house, though, because I knew she was dying to know what I'd found out.

Jenny and Anne were in the kitchen. Anne was still experimenting with corn muffins to get just the right mix so that they were fairly sweet but not too sweet. She was lifting them out of the muffin pan and putting them on a plate.

"Come and try this latest batch," she said. "I've used smaller pans and put fresh kernels in them."

"I met my birth mother," I said.

Anne stopped lifting the muffins out of the pan and looked at me.

"You did?" Jenny said. "You mean she was right there at the lawyer's office?"

"Yes," I said.

"What was she like?"

"She *was* the lawyer."

"Wow!" Jenny said.

"Do you remember that lawyer who was the judge at the debating tournament when I won my trophy?"

"The witch? Sure. She sounded terrible. I just hope she never judges a debate I'm in."

"She's my birth mother," I said.

Anne dropped the muffin pan in the sink with a clatter. Then they stared at me and nobody said anything for ages. I guess they didn't know what to say.

"Oh, poor Ellen," Jenny said.

"Maybe she's not so bad when you get to know her," Anne said. "People are often different when they're on the job."

"That's true," Jenny said. "You know how some teachers are horrible at school but nice when you meet them in the grocery store."

"I don't want to get to know her," I said, "and I don't think she wants to know me. She'd have thrown us out of the office if Dad hadn't started yelling at her."

"Your dad yelled at her?"

So I told them how she said having me was sordid, and how Dad had sent me away, and we'd heard his voice all the way down the hall in the waiting room until they came out and then we all talked for a while.

"Goodness, Ellen!" Anne said.

"I feel terrible that I encouraged you to find her," Jenny said. "Big mistake!"

"Well, I was curious," I said. "I kept imagining that she might be a murderer or poor or rich or someone from another country. But I never imagined anything like she is. It couldn't be worse. At least I know now."

"Also you know that you haven't inherited any diseases," Jenny said.

"But maybe I've inherited her nasty disposition," I said. "You know what a bad temper I have. Maybe I'll be mean like her when I grow up."

"Well, you can work on that," Jenny said. "It's not like an incurable disease."

"I think you should just put it behind you now," Anne said. "Have a muffin."

"Let's take some and eat them on the beach," Jenny said.

So we wrapped some muffins up in a napkin and walked down past the marina to the beach. We sat on my rock eating them. It was a bright sunny day and the tide was going out. A lot of people had taken their boats out. The sailboats bobbed up and down on the waves and motorboats zoomed between them.

Kids were playing at the water's edge, collecting seaweed and shells and stuff in little pails. Their voices carried a long way on the still air. They mingled with the cries of the seabirds flying overhead. The air smelled of rotting fish, but it was a seaside smell that I liked.

I decided to put my birth mother out of my mind like Anne said. After all, nothing had changed in my life since the day before yesterday. Then I didn't know anything about my birth mother. Now I did, but it didn't make any difference. I wasn't going to see her ever again.

I began to feel a whole lot better. At least, that is, until I went home.

"Ellen," Dad said when I started to help with supper, "I had a call from Sarah Maslin this morning."

"Oh, no!"

"There's been a new development."

"What does she want?" I said.

"It seems she decided to tell her mother about our meeting. The mother—your grandmother—wants to meet you. She knew nothing about your existence before. She would like you to go over there and visit her as soon as possible."

"Well, I'm not going," I said.

"I think you should," Dad said. "The mother may be quite different from the daughter. As a matter of fact, Sarah Maslin herself sounded a bit different this time around. She apologized for her rudeness the other day. She said that learning about you so suddenly had left her in shock. In any case, as I said, the mother is probably a nicer person. It's a point in her favor that she's so eager to meet you."

"I don't care," I said. "I don't want to see any of them again. I've decided to put all this birth-mother stuff behind me. Anyway, I've already got Gran. That's about as much as I can handle in the grandmother department just now."

"You have to remember, Ellen, that you were the one who set all this in motion. It's entirely your own doing. It seems unreasonable that you should seek out your birth family, and then suddenly when you've got Sarah Maslin and her family all stirred up, you want nothing more to do with them. Besides, I already said you'd go."

"Without even asking me?"

"Well, yes," Dad said. "You weren't here to ask."

"Great! When are we supposed to go?"

"I won't be going with you this time. I told Sarah that I would drive you to the ferry. She'll pick you up at the other end and drive you to her mother's house for lunch. Then she'll drive you back to the ferry afterwards."

"And you'll meet me when I get off the ferry after this lunch?"

"I thought you could take the bus back home."

"So it's all arranged without asking me?"

"Once again, I have to remind you that all this was your doing."

"Won't Sarah Maslin lose a lot of billable hours at her law office while she's carting me to and from the ferry?"

"It's on Sunday. Next Sunday."

"But Gran'll be up for lunch. I thought we weren't going to mention any of this to her."

"I suppose we'll have to tell her sooner or later."

"Well, it's not fair," I yelled. "I don't want to spend Sunday on the ferry by myself and then wait for ages at the bus stop and come home on the bus by myself. And I don't want to meet my horrible birth mother and her horrible mother. And I won't be tossed around like a piece of garbage from one person to the next. And I'm not helping with supper. I'm going over to Jenny's."

"As you wish," he said, as I stomped out of the house.

14

SARAH MET ME in her big car when I got off the ferry at Horseshoe Bay and drove me to her mother's house. It felt weird being alone with her, and I think she felt weird being with me. There was nothing I wanted to talk to her about, and I think she felt the same way.

"Did you enjoy the ferry ride?" she said after we'd been driving for a while.

"I like it better when I'm with someone," I said. "Last year I came over with our debating coach to the provincial tournament. The one you judged."

"I got roped in to judge more than one," she said. She sounded as if she didn't like judging debates.

We pulled into the driveway of a small bungalow and I saw a face at the window.

My grandmother came hurrying to the door. She had gray hair like Gran, but it wasn't curled around her face. It was drawn back into a kind of bun. She was smaller than Gran and dressed all in black.

"So this is Ellen," she said. "Come and let me look at you, child."

She put her hands on my arms and looked at me very hard. I hate being stared at, and I wondered if she thought I was ugly. I was all dressed up in the clothes Jenny had lent me when I visited Mrs. Roscoe-Jones, but my hair had got blown around on the ferry. Maybe she was used to that, though, because Sarah's hair was always all over the place, too.

My grandmother gripped me very tight, and she stared at me for a long time.

"Rachel," she said to Sarah. "It's Rachel she looks like."

"I knew you'd say that," Sarah said.

"The same eyes she has. The same hair," my grandmother said. "Bring the photograph out of my bedroom."

I was getting used to people talking about me as if I wasn't there.

"She doesn't want to look at old photos," Sarah said. "She's hungry. She came on the ferry and she hasn't eaten in hours."

"That's good. Never eat anything on the ferry," my grandmother said. "You could get very sick. You could get food poisoning."

"Oh, sure," Sarah said. "When the ferry comes in, they're always taking people off in ambulances because they've been poisoned by eating hot dogs and hamburgers."

Actually, Dad had given me money for food. I'd had clam chowder and pie and ice cream and I wasn't even hungry.

"Who's Rachel?" I said.

"She was my older sister. She died," my grandmother said.

"I'm sorry," I said.

"Oh, that was years and years ago in Poland," Sarah said. "It's water under the bridge, though you wouldn't know it in this house."

"It seems like yesterday to me," my grandmother said.

"Everything seems like yesterday to you," Sarah said. "Let's have some lunch."

The house was very small and dark and the carpets and chairs were old and worn out like ours at home, but the dining room had a big table with a lace tablecloth and brass candlesticks in the middle. It was set for four people.

My grandmother sat opposite me. She was still

staring at me, but I didn't mind because she had a smile on her face as if she liked me.

Sarah went out and came back helping a very old man who shuffled to the table slowly using a walker. He was dressed in black, too, and he was wearing a hat. It was the person in the photograph in Sarah's office. She got him settled in his chair, put a cushion behind his back, rolled up his sleeves and tied a big white napkin around his neck. He looked at the food on the table before he caught sight of me.

"Is that the girl Sarah's going to adopt?" he said. He had an accent and it was hard to make out what he was saying.

Sarah laughed. It was the first time I'd seen her laugh, and she looked a lot nicer when she did.

"No, Zayde. This is Ellen, your great-granddaughter."

My grandmother said something to him in a foreign language. Then he bowed his head and said a string of words I didn't understand. It sounded as if he was saying grace the way Mrs. T., our old housekeeper, did.

"He gets mixed up," my grandmother said when he'd finished. "Most of the time he doesn't know where he is."

"He's a sweetheart," Sarah said. "Eat up, Zayde."

"You should be married," he said, shaking his head sadly. "It's too late already."

The meat was lamb and he just pushed it around on his plate. I ate a small piece. I didn't like lamb even when I was hungry. My grandmother dumped a big dollop of potatoes on my plate without asking me.

"Don't keep pushing food on her," Sarah said.

"She gets very irritable with me," my grandmother said to me.

They sounded exactly like Mum and Gran, the way they bickered all the time.

"Would you like something else to drink? Some juice you'd like?" my grandmother said. There was just a glass of water by my plate.

"Could I please have a glass of milk?" I said.

"Milk?" Zayde said in a shocked voice. "She asks for milk?" He looked at my grandmother as if I'd asked for a bottle of beer. My grandmother looked a bit startled as well. I wondered if she thought milk gave you food poisoning, too.

"Oh, for Pete's sake," Sarah said. "She can have milk if she wants. What difference does it make?"

She went out, got a big glass of milk and set it in front of me with a thud. My grandmother just shrugged, but the old man put his knife and fork down and stared at it.

Whenever my grandmother said something, Sarah said something rude, but every time Zayde said something, Sarah smiled at him. She tried to encourage him to eat some more. He wasn't doing very well with his lunch. He had a tattoo on his arm but it wasn't the usual kind with flowers or birds. It was a row of numbers. He saw me looking at it.

"You were in the camps?" he said.

"I never went to camp," I said. "It's pretty expensive. My friend Jenny did, though. In Saskatchewan. A camp for artists."

"She got out?" he said.

"She came home early." Then I stopped when I remembered why she came home. I didn't know what to say next. "She didn't mind," I said. "There were bagpipers in the camp."

"Bagpipes?"

"It was also a music camp, actually."

"Music," he said. "The children made the music! They made the opera!" He shook his head very sadly and put his knife and fork down altogether. It was obvious he wasn't going to eat any more.

"I told you we wouldn't want a big meal," Sarah said to her mother.

"Could I help with the dishes?" I said after she'd taken Zayde back to his room.

"I'll see to them," Sarah said. "You just sit and chat with my mother."

"I'd like to see a picture of Rachel who I look like," I said to my grandmother.

"Come," she said, and we went down the hallway to her room. There was a bed, and a dresser and photographs in frames on the dresser and all over the walls. They were mostly black and white, though some were faded and yellow.

She took a large photograph of a girl in a silver frame off the dresser and handed it to me. The girl was older than me but she did look a lot like me, even though she was wearing old-fashioned clothes. She had dark springy hair and glasses with round rims. My grandmother and I sat side by side on the bed looking at the picture.

"You know that you're Jewish now, don't you, Ellen?"

"Yes," I said. "My dad told me."

"Because your mother is Jewish, you are a Jew. You are entitled to become a citizen if you go to Israel. Would you like to go to Israel, Ellen?"

"I don't know," I said. "I don't know anything about Israel. It's probably expensive to fly there."

"It's the homeland of the Jewish people. I shall go there one day soon. Perhaps you will come with me."

"I'd like to," I said. "I like traveling."

"Good. In the Jewish faith we name our children after the dear departed ones," she said. "You should be called Rachel."

"It's a nice name."

"So. I shall call you Rachel," she said.

"What shall I call you?" I said.

"I'm your Grandma Rebecca," she said. "But you can call me Bubba."

"Tell me what Rachel was like."

"She was very gifted. Very gifted in many ways. She played the piano…" She fumbled around for another picture and found one of Rachel playing the piano. She was older in this picture and her hair was longer and tied back, but some of it had got loose around her face. She looked really pretty in a long dress.

"I play the piano," I said. "I've been taking lessons for over a year."

"Wonderful, wonderful," my grandmother said. "I wanted Sarah to play but she wouldn't practice. Everything I wanted her to do, she refused. I don't know why that was, do you?"

"Sometimes people don't like being told what to do all the time," I said. "Do you have any more pictures of Rachel?"

"There's a chest full of pictures under this bed. When you come back, we'll look at them together. I'll get the piano tuned also, and you can play for me."

"Okay," I said.

"See," she said to Sarah as we were leaving,

"Rachel wants soon to come back. We have many things to talk about. She should come for the whole weekend so that I can take her to synagogue."

"Her dad isn't going to like that," Sarah said. "And he's not someone you want to tangle with."

"You don't have to come back," Sarah said, while we were waiting for the ferry to come in. "It must have been very boring for you."

"No," I said. I suddenly realized I really wanted to see Grandma Rebecca again. "I like Bubba. She's going to tell me what it was like when she and Rachel were growing up in Poland."

"You're sure you want to hear about all that?" Sarah said. "It's pretty depressing. I couldn't stand it when I was your age."

"Yes, I do want to hear it," I said. "Thanks for taking me. Will you pick me up at the ferry again next time?"

"I guess so," she said with a sigh. "Your dad has my phone number. You'll have to square it with him."

She didn't sound too thrilled about the idea.

15

I LIKED MY new grandmother a lot, and I got to like Sarah a bit better after the first time, though I still couldn't think of her as my mother. But at least now we had a lot to talk about when we were waiting for the ferry to come in. There was a waiting room for foot passengers but she didn't want me to go in there by myself, so I sat in the car until we heard the boarding announcement. Often she explained words I didn't understand or things that had puzzled me at lunch.

Bubba was always at the window looking out for me when we arrived, and she ran to open the door as we walked up the path. There was a little silver box nailed to the right side of the door. Bubba said it was a mezuzah and there was a tiny paper inside it with verses from the Torah. She'd taught me the words that observant Jews say when they come to a house. I liked the words, so I always touched the mezuzah and said, "How goodly are thy tents, O Jacob, and thy tabernacles, O Israel!" Then she gave me a big hug.

I generally arrived in time for lunch, and I didn't eat anything on the ferry on the way over because she liked me to eat a lot. She thought I was too thin and she seemed to think they didn't give me enough to eat at home. Sometimes, when it was just the three of us, we ate in the kitchen. But I liked it when Zayde came to the table, even though he stared at me and said weird things. When he was there he always put Sarah in a good mood.

He got used to seeing me at the table but he never figured out who I was. Sometimes he thought Sarah had adopted me because I was an orphan. Once he called me a kaddish.

"She's Rachel," he said more than once.

"Rachel's dead," Bubba said.

Sometimes he said I was Rachel's girl.

"Ellen, do you know about the concentration camps?" Sarah asked me as we waited for the ferry.

"Yes," I said. "I read the diary of Anne Frank. It's one of my favorite books."

"Did you know that all the people who entered the camps had numbers tattooed on their skin?"

"No. Is that why Zayde got upset when I talked about Jenny's camp and the bagpipers?"

Then Sarah told me about a concentration camp called Theresienstadt, where the little kids had put on an opera. One performance was planned to trick the Red Cross inspectors and other visitors into thinking the camp was a nice place for Jews to live. But after they'd performed the opera and the inspectors had left, the composer and all the children were shipped off to another camp and killed.

The opera is still performed in the memory of all the children who died. It's called *Brundibar*. Sarah said that whenever the opera comes to Vancouver, my grandmother sees it. Next time, she would take me with her.

"Why did Zayde call me a radish?"

"Not radish, kaddish. That's the prayer children say at the grave of their parents and for eleven months afterwards. Long ago in the old country, people who didn't have children would adopt a boy so there'd be someone to recite the prayer when they died. And he was called their kaddish."

Often the ferry came in and I had to leave before I could ask all the questions I wanted to.

Sarah explained the laws of kosher food, and I learned that meat and dairy products like milk and cheese couldn't be eaten together. So I knew why Zayde was shocked when I asked for a glass of milk.

"Well, I won't drink milk with my lunch again," I said.

"You don't have to worry about that," she said. "I don't keep kosher. It's just the strictly religious Jews who do."

"It upsets Zayde," I said. "So I won't do it."

"Well, as you wish," she said, smiling. "See you soon, Ellen."

Because it was the end of the summer, the ferries were usually running on time. I often wished there'd be a delay so that we could talk for longer. It's a lot easier to ask questions when you're sitting beside someone in a car than it is when they're looking right at you. I had so many questions I wanted to ask Sarah.

I was trying to get up the courage to ask about myself—how I got to be born, why she gave me away. But there were lots of other things, too. I was really curious about Rachel, who was my great-aunt. Bubba talked about her and showed me pictures, but she would never tell me what had happened to her.

"Did my great-aunt Rachel have any kids?" I asked Sarah one day.

"No," she said. "At least not as far as we know."

"Maybe," Bubba said, when I asked her. "Maybe she did."

"I've noticed you squint when you're reading the signs at the terminal," Sarah said when the ferry was late one day.

"I don't have good eyesight," I said.

"I don't, either," she said.

"But you don't wear glasses."

"I have contact lenses," she said. "Don't you get your eyes tested regularly?"

"Not really. Besides, Mum couldn't take us because she was ill, and Dad had his hands full looking after Mum and the twins."

"Look, Ellen," she said, "I'm going to make an appointment for you to see my eye doctor. I hope your dad won't mind."

"He won't mind, but I won't have time to see a doctor when I'm in Vancouver."

"I've already talked to your dad about Rosh Hashanah. My mother wants you with her for the whole weekend, and your dad says it's okay."

"What's Rosh Hashanah?"

"It's the Jewish New Year and it's one of the most important days in the Jewish calendar. My mother would like you to come to synagogue with us. You can see the eye doctor on the Friday."

"I thought you didn't go to synagogue," I said.

"I go on the high holy days," she said. "Everyone does. You're welcome to stay at my condo. You'd have your own bedroom and bathroom, and I think you'd like it better than sleeping on the couch at my mother's place."

"I think Bubba would be disappointed if I didn't stay with her. Besides, I like staying at the house because I can look at her pictures and listen to her stories."

"You're right, she would be disappointed. Well, there's the boarding announcement. Run along, Ellen."

16

IT MUST SEEM strange to be celebrating the New Year in the fall," Sarah said.

"Not really," I said. "It always feels like a new year when school starts up again."

This year it felt like a new year for other reasons, too. I'd found a new family. In a way, I was a different person. I even looked different.

Sarah drove straight from the ferry to the eye doctor, who tested my eyes and gave me a prescription for new glasses. The doctor asked me if I wanted contact lenses now or if I wanted to wait until I was older.

"Get some regular glasses and contacts as well to see if you can manage them," Sarah said.

"Wouldn't it be too expensive?" I said.

"Don't worry about that," Sarah said. "It's my New Year's gift to you. I've settled it with your dad."

I decided to wait till I was older to get contacts, so we went to a wall covered with different kinds of glasses and I tried on lots of pairs. Sarah and the assistant helped me pick out the ones that suited me best. They had no frames and I looked as if I was hardly wearing glasses at all. I was really happy with them because they made me look so good.

Then the assistant said they wouldn't be ready for five days.

I guess I looked pretty let down because Sarah turned to the assistant.

"That's not good enough," she said. "We need them tomorrow. Put a rush on them. If you can't do them overnight, we'll cancel the order. And have them sent out to me by courier."

"Well, I'll see what we can do," the assistant said.

"Don't just see. Do it!" Sarah said. "Come along, Ellen. You'll have your glasses tomorrow."

The assistant looked at me as if to say, you poor thing with a bossy mother like that. I wouldn't want to be you.

As usual, Bubba was at the window looking out for us when we drove up.

"*Leshana tova tikosevu,* Rachel," she said, as she

opened the door. "May you be remembered for a good year! May you be inscribed in the Book of Life!"

She told me that the Book of Life was opened on Rosh Hashanah and the names of all the righteous people were written in it. She gave me a Jewish calendar with all the Jewish holidays in it, and all the Hebrew names of the months, beginning with Elul.

I went to the synagogue the next day feeling very good in my new glasses. Sarah had also bought me a new dress with a matching jacket, and some new shoes. Zayde came along in his wheelchair. When Sarah got him out of the car outside the synagogue, there were lots of people on the sidewalk. They crowded around Zayde, greeting him in Hebrew. He nodded happily, though he probably couldn't hear a word they said.

As I walked out after the service, I heard someone call my name.

"Ellen Fremedon, is that you?"

It was a familar voice, and when I turned around I saw Spotz.

"Spotz!" I said. He looked a lot older than he did the last time I saw him because he was wearing a suit and a yarmulke.

"I thought it was you when you came in, only

you look different. By the way, I'm Jonathan in Vancouver."

"I'm Rachel in Vancouver," I said. "You look different, too. What are you doing here?"

"This is my family's synagogue."

"It's my family's synagogue, too," I said. "I came with my mother and grandma and Zayde."

"Your mother?" he said. "But Jenny told me your mother...I sent you a card..."

"You did?"

"You didn't get it?"

"I didn't see all the cards," I said. "I'm sorry."

"I don't understand," he said, "about your mother."

"I was adopted," I said. "It's my birth mother I came with today."

"Your birth mother?"

"Sarah Maslin's my birth mother."

"Sarah Maslin!"

Just then one of the girls who was standing nearby started pulling at Spotz's sleeve, trying to drag him away. I thought she must be his girlfriend. She was very rude.

He must have told her Sarah was my mother because she and another girl turned around and stared at me as I walked out.

I felt so mixed up I didn't even say goodbye. I

walked out to Sarah's car and climbed into the back with Zayde. Bubba rode in front with Sarah.

"Who was that boy Rachel was talking to?" she said.

"The Davidson boy," Sarah said. "He and Debbie used to live in Partridge Cove, you remember. Apparently he went to Ellen's school."

"Have you lost your appetite?" Bubba said to me at lunch. "You're so quiet."

She'd been telling me that we had apples and honey on the table to symbolize our hope for a sweet year ahead, and that the two round loaves of challah were a symbol of good fortune, but I wasn't paying attention.

"She's probably tired out from the service," Sarah said. "It's so long and it can be very off-putting the first time."

"It wasn't off-putting," I said. "I liked it."

It was true. I liked the chants and the words and I really liked the blowing of the shofar. My grandmother had told me the story of Abraham, and how he'd been willing to sacrifice his son Isaac to show how obedient he was to God. But luckily God decided he could sacrifice a ram instead. That's why the ram's horn is blown on the high holidays.

But actually I was thinking about Spotz. As soon as I got home to Partridge Cove, I wanted to look for all the cards Gran had put away and find the one he'd sent me.

I was helping my grandmother with the dishes after lunch, when the phone rang. Bubba came back and said it was for me.

It was Spotz.

"Hi, Ellen!" he said. "Or am I supposed to call you Rachel?"

"Bubba calls me that," I said. "You can, too, if you want."

"I wanted to apologize about this morning," he said. "I was so surprised to see you and then my cousins dragged me off. They're a menace, those two."

"That's okay," I said. "I was surprised, too."

"Have you joined the debating society this year?"

"No. There's too much going on in my life just now. I'm just getting used to my new family and everything."

"There's a youth group at the synagogue," he said. "It's a lot of fun. You should join."

"I only come over on weekends, and not every weekend," I said.

"Well, give me a call when you come over again."

"Okay," I said.

That was one more surprise to get used to in my new life. At the end of school last year I'd been sad because I thought I'd never see Spotz again. Now he'd suddenly appeared and asked me to call him the next time I was in Vancouver.

As soon as I got back home, I planned to go down to Somecot, lock the door and write a long letter to Mum telling her all about it.

17

IT WAS DAD who invited Grandma Rebecca to visit us. He arranged it with Sarah. Without asking me, of course.

"By the way," he said at lunch one day, "Sarah tells me her mother is eager to meet the rest of us. I've invited her to come for lunch a week from Sunday."

"She won't be able to," I said. "She doesn't drive and she doesn't like the ferry."

"She's already accepted," he said. "Sarah will drive her over."

"Will Zayde come, too?"

"I understand that Sarah's grandfather is too frail to travel far, though I did include him in the invitation, of course."

Bubba was always asking me what my brothers and my father were like. She often said, "I'd like to meet your other family and see your little house in the garden." But I never expected it to happen. I thought my two families would always be separate — one in Vancouver and one in Partridge Cove — and I'd travel back and forth between them.

I didn't like this new development one bit.

"I don't know why those people have suddenly decided to take such an interest in Ellen after ignoring her all these years," Gran said.

Gran had a habit of calling Sarah and Grandma Rebecca "those people."

"It was Ellen who made the initial contact with them," Dad said. "She wanted to know about her birth family."

"If I'd been consulted on the matter, I would have told Ellen to put the whole idea out of her mind. It would have been better if she'd left well enough alone. And so soon after her mother passed away, too! I know there's a lot about these reunions on television, but I can't see the point of them myself."

"You don't have to meet them, Mother."

"I think I should be here," Gran said, "to make sure they don't take advantage of Ellen. It's too bad I wasn't told about it at the very beginning."

"How on earth could they take advantage of Ellen?" Dad said.

"Maybe they want to convert her. These people always do. They go door to door with pamphlets."

"No, they don't, Mother. Those are different groups—evangelical Christians, Seventh Day Adventists, Jehovah's Witnesses and so on. Judaism is not a proselytizing religion."

"What's that?" I said.

"It means the Jews don't seek converts. They're very emphatic about that."

"Oh, are they?" Gran said. "Well, it's not very friendly of them to exclude other people. I suppose they think they'll go to heaven, and the rest of us can go to the other place, for all they care."

"Anyone who wants to convert can become Jewish," I said. Bubba had told me the story of Ruth. She married a Jewish man and said, "Wither thou goest, I will go, and thy people will be my people."

"I don't think hell figures largely in the Jewish faith," Dad said.

"You appear to know a lot about this all of a sudden, David. I thought you believed all religions to be irrational. It seems they've got to you already."

"I had only a single brief meeting with Ellen's

birth mother, and I have never met Mrs. Maslin," Dad said.

"Then who was behind this plan to have them over here?"

"I believe it was Mrs. Maslin. She's become very attached to Ellen in the short time she's known her, and she expressed a wish to meet us. There's nothing unreasonable about that, surely."

"So she invited herself! Those people are very pushy. Everybody knows that."

"Mother, really!" Dad said. "I didn't expect to hear that from you. And I wish you wouldn't say such things in front of the children."

"I'm glad she's coming," Tim said. "Everybody in our class has two grandmothers except us. I bet she'll give us presents for Christmas."

"For one thing, she isn't *your* grandmother," I said. "And for another, Jews don't celebrate Christmas, they celebrate Chanukah."

"Well, I hope she brings us a present anyway," Toby said.

"And don't start going on about spiders," I said. "They don't want to hear about Amaryllis eating live crickets or shedding her skin or mating, or doing any of the other disgusting things she does. That would put them off their food for sure."

"She isn't called Amaryllis," Tim said, "She's called Primrose."

"They've asked us not to go to any trouble," Dad said.

"When people ask you not to go to any trouble," Gran said, "that usually means they think you ought to be going to a lot of trouble."

"Well, we shall be having a very simple lunch," Dad said. "I'll get a couple of baguettes from the bakery. There'll be cheese and cold cuts."

"You won't be able to serve pork or ham," Gran said. "I expect you know that since you've become such an expert on the Jewish faith."

"I've already discussed that with Sarah," Dad said. "The cold cuts will be chicken and turkey and smoked salmon. Kelly has promised to make one of her celebrity salads. And I suppose we can count on you to bring your usual excellent cake from the bakery."

"A storebought cake probably won't be good enough for them," Gran said. "I expect I shall have to go to the trouble of baking one."

"Why not bring one of your fruitcakes?" Dad said. "Didn't you make some this year? I thought that was why you took that bottle of Napoleon brandy home."

"Those cakes are for our Christmas celebration," Gran said. "I'd no idea you resented the use of your brandy. I suppose I should have bought a bottle of cheap rum. Not that we have much to celebrate anyway this year. I might just as well offer the cakes to these people."

"What's your grandma in a snit about now?" Kelly said when she came by later. "I've never seen her so mad. Why's she got so uptight about having two people over for lunch?"

It gave me nightmares to think of them all sitting around the table, especially when Gran was in what Mum used to call "one of her moods." I kept imagining a fight breaking out around the table and Bubba going back to Vancouver in a huff and never wanting to see me again. I was dreading the lunch so much that I got a pain in my stomach when I thought about it.

At least Zayde was staying home with Rosa, who helped my grandmother out sometimes. I'd got used to him but I didn't know what he'd make of the twins.

Also, I was worried about Bubba calling me Rachel. I thought Gran would have a fit if she did.

I told Dad how worried I was.

"Gran may say rude things about guests before and after they visit," Dad said, "but I can assure you she will be very polite to their faces."

"It's not just Gran. It's the twins," I said. "Maybe we should ask Kelly and Jake to take them out to a farm or something for the afternoon."

"I'm asking Kelly to help out with the lunch," Dad said. "Besides, Sarah said her mother is especially eager to meet the twins."

I got more and more nervous as Sunday drew nearer.

18

IT WAS TRUE what Dad said about Gran. When the visitors arrived, she rushed to the door and acted like she'd been dying to meet them.

"How wonderful to meet you both at last," she said with a big smile on her face. "Ellen's told us so many good things about you."

Then Bubba said she'd heard many good things about Gran and the twins from me. I couldn't remember saying good things to either of them about each other. And I sure hadn't said anything good about the twins.

They went on saying polite things to each other, while the visitors got their coats off and handed over a bunch of flowers. Bubba gave the twins a box of chocolates. It usually means big trouble when anyone gives the twins one box between the two of them but, of course, she didn't know that. At least they postponed fighting over who got the caramels until later.

When Bubba was settled on the sofa next to Gran, Dad asked her if he could offer her a glass of wine or sherry. She said water would be fine.

"Wine I find too activating," she told Gran. "On special occasions, yes. But drinking wine so much. This I don't understand at all."

"Oh, I agree with you entirely," Gran said. "The younger generation seems to seize any excuse to drink these days. It's no wonder there are so many health problems—diabetes, and drunk driving, and multiple cirrhosis and so on."

"Sarah," Dad said, "are you willing to put your health on the line by joining me in a glass of wine?"

"Oh, definitely," Sarah said.

Ever since she'd shaken Dad's hand, she'd looked at him nervously, as though she thought he might fly into a temper. She'd often asked me about him. Did he get angry often? Did he ever get violent? I wondered if she thought I'd been abused or something. I thought he must be trying to make up for yelling at her in her office by being extra polite. She relaxed a bit after he gave her the wine.

Bubba and Gran started talking about various

friends of theirs who'd had to wait for months for surgeries. Dad was telling Sarah about the local wineries. The twins were looking at the pictures of chocolates that came with the box and deciding which ones they wanted. Nobody was paying any attention to me so I went into the kitchen and helped Kelly. We set all the salads and platters on the table. Then Kelly went in and told them lunch was ready.

"What beautiful coloring you have, my dear," Bubba said to Kelly. "Don't you think so, Sarah?"

Sarah looked as if she couldn't care less.

"My hair's the same color," Tim said.

"No, it isn't," I said. "Yours is orange like a carrot. Your freckles are, too. Kelly's is chestnut-colored."

"All this praise of Kelly's appearance is going to make her vain," Gran said.

"There's no danger of that," Dad said. "Kelly is endowed with a very pleasant disposition. She couldn't put up with us the way she does, otherwise."

I'd never heard so much polite conversation in our house before. It was like we were all acting in a play, and it was giving me a bit of a headache.

When we sat down at the table, Bubba said what a wonderful view of the inlet we had. She said we were very lucky in our location.

"I'm afraid our luck is about to run out," Dad said.

"That is not possible, surely!" Bubba said. "From such a lovely place you're planning to move away?"

"No," Dad said. "But the place is going to be very changed if the developers get their wish. They are hoping to replace the marina and build a hotel, a restaurant, a casino, and a series of high-rise housing units along our waterfront. Our days as a quiet rural community may be numbered."

"But surely there's opposition to such a development?" Sarah said.

"There's some opposition, but it's limited to a very small group of us. We're not optimistic that we can resist the change. We learned how difficult that is when we tried to stop a developer from putting a subdivision on top of our aquifer some time ago."

"But things have changed recently," Sarah said. "People have become much more aware of the need to preserve water and protect the natural environment."

"True," Dad said. "But our resources are limited. It's hard to fight the developers and their high-powered, money-grubbing lawyers."

As soon as he said it, he realized that he'd insulted her, and so did everybody else. There was a long silence, and we all concentrated really hard on our food for a while.

End of polite conversation, I thought. This family doesn't have enough practice at it.

"Some female spiders eat the male spiders after they've mated," Tim said after a while.

"Praying mantises do that," Toby said. "But they don't eat the whole mate. They just bite its head off. It can go on mating even when its head's bitten off."

"It mates even harder when its head's gone and — " Tim said.

"That's enough of that," Dad said.

Sarah put down her fork and drank some more wine.

"Since she was a child my daughter fears spiders very much," Bubba said.

"I had a dear friend who felt much the same about snakes," Gran said. "It became an obsession, and she had to be treated by hypnosis. It was not very successful, unfortunately."

"How terrible!" Bubba said. "A woman I know had migraine headaches. For her, too, hypnosis was tried. Her suffering was very great and then she passed away. "

"I'd like to see your marina," Sarah said to Dad. "Perhaps I can give you some help in this business with the developer."

"I'd be happy to take you down there after lunch," Dad said. "It's a short walk, as long as you're wearing sensible shoes."

"I always wear sensible shoes," she said, but she was smiling.

We finally got back on the polite track when Kelly brought in Gran's cake. Bubba said it was the best she'd tasted in a long time and that fruitcake was one of her favorites. When Gran said she'd made it, Bubba asked if Gran would be willing to share the recipe. Gran said she'd be delighted.

After lunch Dad and Sarah went down to the marina, and I showed Bubba the garden and Somecot. Gran said she'd help Kelly with the dishes.

When we came up from the garden, Gran had wrapped up the rest of the fruitcake for Bubba to take home. Bubba said that was too generous and she couldn't possibly accept it, but Gran insisted. They went back and forth like that for about a million years, and Bubba ended up taking the cake.

Then Bubba said she had a little specialty of her own that she'd like to share with Gran, although it was not as good as the fruitcake. It was called rugelach, and she made it for Chanukah.

When Dad and Sarah came back from the marina, they were talking very seriously.

"You've been going about this in entirely the

wrong way," Sarah said. "You need to check the developer's previous projects — every single one of them, no matter what country they're in. Some developers have very suspicious track records."

They sat down at the table and Dad brought out a clipboard and pen. He wrote down all Sarah's suggestions. It was weird seeing Dad taking instructions and having someone telling him he was wrong.

"I can see I have a lot to learn about the laws that apply to local governments," Dad said.

"Well, I'd be willing to come and make a presentation at the next meeting of your concerned citizens' group," Sarah said.

"We have very limited financial resources, I'm afraid," Dad said.

"This kind of project interests me a lot," Sarah said. "It would be pro bono."

"What's pro bono?" I said.

"It would be done without a fee. Most lawyers do some pro bono work. We aren't all the money-grubbers some people believe us to be."

"Quite," Dad said, looking sheepish. "But our meetings are on weekday evenings."

"Then I'll charter a floatplane," she said.

"A floatplane. Wow!" Tim said.

When Bubba heard that Gran was going back to

the city on the bus, she said it would be no inconvenience at all for them to drive her home on their way back to the ferry. Gran said if they had the time to come in for a moment, she could give Grandma Rebecca the recipe. In fact, perhaps they could have a cup of tea with her. She'd love nothing better.

They all went out to Sarah's car and Bubba said Gran should take the front seat. Gran said the back seat would be fine. They argued back and forth until I started to wonder whether they'd ever actually leave, but Gran ended up riding in front next to Sarah.

"Well, that wasn't as bad as you expected, was it?" Kelly said after we'd all waved them off, and the car was finally headed down the road to the city.

"Far from it," Dad said. "Sarah gave me some very valuable advice. I can see that having a lawyer in the family — as it were — is quite an asset."

Everyone seemed very pleased with the lunch, but I was so exhausted that I had to go and lie down.

19

DAD WASN'T THE only one who thought that having a lawyer in the family was a useful thing.

"When shall we see Sarah again?" Gran asked the next Sunday.

Dad looked up in surprise. We knew Gran had been talking to Bubba on the phone and sending her recipes and knitting patterns, but she wasn't as keen on Sarah. She thought she should show more respect for her mother.

"Do you want another ride in her car?" Toby said.

"No," Gran said. "But I've been thinking ever since Elinor passed away that I should make a new will. I'd like Sarah to help me."

"What's a will?" Tim said.

"It's a document in which you declare who will inherit your possessions after your death," Dad said.

"What happens if you don't have one?" Toby said.

"Then your possessions go to your next of kin."

"What's next of kin?" Tim said.

"Your nearest relatives. In your case, that would be me or Toby or Ellen."

"Ellen?" Tim said. "I don't want Ellen getting my stuff. I'd better make a will right away."

"Don't worry," I said. "I don't want any of your junk. I might end up with a tarantula."

"I don't want you getting my night-light and my watch with the dial that lights up in the dark."

"You don't need to pay big bucks to a lawyer to make a will," Kelly said. "You can get kits in the drugstore that tell you how to write your own. They cost $6.95. My mum got one."

Soon the twins had forms all over the table with THIS IS THE LAST WILL AND TESTAMENT across the top. They were quite complicated and Dad refused to have anything to do with them, so Kelly was helping. They were leaving most of their stuff to her and to Thumper Higginson.

Sarah wouldn't help with Gran's will, either. I asked her about it one day as we waited for the ferry.

"Lawyers can't draw up wills for people they're related to, even distantly," she said.

Sarah didn't seem to have any objections helping Dad fight against the marina development, though. Just as she promised, she came over by floatplane to address the community meeting.

Word must have got around that a big-shot lawyer was coming from the mainland, because the community center was packed. All our friends —Kelly, Jake, Anne, Cathy, Jenny, Mr. and Mrs. Banks, Higg and others—were there. But there were lots who were in favor of the marina development, too. Dad had warned Sarah that the audience might not be exactly friendly.

"I'm quite accustomed to the rough and tumble," she said. "A court room isn't exactly a tea party, you know."

Even though Sarah is not very big, she has a strong voice that makes people sit up and pay attention. So everyone listened very quietly while she was speaking. Nobody made rude jokes or heckled the way they usually do at meetings, but I saw some of them roll their eyes a few times when they didn't like what they were hearing.

She began by talking about our rights as taxpayers. She said that the community planners and directors were obliged by law to consult with experts about the effect of this development on the water table that supports our wells and feeds the rivers that are important salmon habitats. Under the Freedom of Information act, every taxpayer has the right to see the reports by experts on the water, sewage, traffic and the environment.

She talked about the various ways of breaking the law. She warned the planners and directors and members of the water board that if they made decisions, either knowingly or through negligence, that harmed the community, they would be held responsible. Severe penalties could be imposed on them.

Then she took up conflict of interest. You were in conflict of interest if you supported the development when you, or any member of your family, stood to gain money from it. If any city planners or members of the water board found themselves in that position, they should step down.

"Wherever there are millions and millions of dollars at stake, the potential for conflict of interest, bribery and double dealing is very high. But bear in mind that the penalties for bribery and corruption are also very severe."

She paused and asked if anyone had any questions. There was silence for a while. I guess everybody found her too scary to say anything. Then I nearly fell off my seat when I saw Toby's hand shoot up.

"I have a question," he said. "Suppose a person has a tarantula and it bites someone. Could the person be thrown in jail?"

Some people laughed, but Sarah answered him really seriously. She said that if someone owns a dangerous animal—whether it's a tarantula or a pitbull—and that animal attacks someone, the owner is indeed liable.

I guess Toby's question gave people more nerve because a lot of them raised their hands and asked questions after that. They were still asking questions when the meeting ended.

We were going to walk home, because Dad had to drive Sarah back to her floatplane. They left by a side door and the rest of the hall emptied slowly because there were so many people. I heard a lot of different remarks as I joined the line to get out the door.

"That lady lawyer sure knows her stuff," someone said.

"Wish I'd hired her when I was up on that DUI charge."

"Bet she makes a bundle."

"Chartered a plane to get over here."

"Heard some of them guys charge five hundred bucks an hour."

Then I heard something that stopped me dead in my tracks.

"Hope that floatplane goes down," someone said in a kind of whisper.

"Maybe it can be arranged."

"That or something else."

I spun around quickly but the crowd was thinning into single and double file to get through the doors. Mr. and Mrs. Banks were right behind me. They smiled at me and I could tell they hadn't heard the scary remarks. There was no way I could tell who the whisperers were.

Outside the hall I met up with Kelly and Jake and the twins and we all walked back to the house.

"If Primrose bit somebody, do you think Sarah would get me out of prison free bono?" Tim said.

"It's *pro* bono," I said. "And I don't see why she'd bother, so you'd better buy that thing a stronger cage."

Dad was already back when we walked in.

"That went very well, don't you think?" he said. "I wish we'd had that kind of help when we were trying to save the aquifer."

"I'm going to suggest that our tribal council get her to help us," Jake said. "There's a developer trying to put a subdivision on top of our ancestral burying site."

"She has a bossy way of talking," Kelly said. "People don't like that in a woman. You could see a lot of them were getting their dander up."

She was in the kitchen making a pot of coffee.

"Mrs. Fenwick said she was shrill," I said.

"I think she has a fine speaking voice," Jake said.

"She's certainly an effective speaker," Dad said.

Then I told them about what I'd heard as I was leaving the hall. Dad and Jake looked at each other.

"She should know about that," Dad said. "I have her home phone number. She'll be home shortly and I think Ellen should tell her exactly what she heard."

So after a while, we all crowded into Dad's study. He has a speakerphone so we could talk at the same time. He punched in her number and asked her if she'd got back home safely.

"Well, of course, I did, David," she said. "Why shouldn't I? I wasn't exactly crossing the Atlantic in a balloon."

"Seriously, Sarah," Dad said. "Ellen heard something very alarming. Here she is to tell you about it."

So I told her about the voice that said it would be easy to arrange for the floatplane to go down, or for something like that to happen.

"Threats of that kind are very common in my

job," she said. "Lawyers are often subject to attempts to intimidate them. We take note of the threats but we don't let them bother us too much. And we certainly don't let them influence our work."

"Do you have a security system in your apartment?" Jake said. He'd worked as a security guard at a mall.

"I do have a security system. I also have some training in martial arts," she said. "It's good of you to be concerned, but please don't worry. It's late and we're all tired. Get a good night's sleep, all of you."

The phone clicked off.

"I wouldn't like to think that helping us has put her in danger," Dad said.

"She could use a bodyguard," Jake said.

"Why don't you apply for the job?" Kelly said.

"Don't you be so snarky!" Jake said.

"She's a very brave woman," Dad said.

"She's scared of spiders," Tim said.

"Those two think she hung the moon," Kelly said as we carried the coffee mugs into the kitchen.

Kelly was jealous of Sarah, and Tim didn't like her much. I was getting to like her better than I did at first, and I sure didn't want anything bad to happen to her. It was true she had a gruff way of talking that made her seem rude, but she could be quite nice underneath. Like Dad and Jake, I was a bit worried.

20

GRADUALLY THE EXCITEMENT died down and things got back to normal. At least as normal as they ever got around our place. The twins now had something on their minds besides spiders. They were always changing their wills, and they got a paperback book off the library rack called *The Legal System for Dummies.*

"It must have been written specially for you," I said.

At Bubba's house, Zayde had got used to seeing me at the lunch table. One day he took a handful of nuts out of his pocket and put them next to my plate. Then he went to his chair and sat watching me.

"They're pine nuts," Bubba said. "He bought

them for us when we were girls long ago in Poland."

"Thank you, Zayde," I said. They tasted stale.

"See, he likes you," Bubba said.

But I don't think he did. He often scowled when he saw me at the table, and he always stared at me for a long time.

"It's because you keep calling her Rachel," Sarah said. "Of course he gets mixed up. Her name's Ellen."

There was so much to do at Bubba's house. After we'd eaten lunch, Zayde went to sleep and Sarah drove off to do errands. I played the piano for Bubba, and sometimes she played music for me on her old record player. We both liked Chopin. I'd found music in the piano bench that had the name Fryderyk Szopen across the top. She said that was Chopin's name in Polish. She told me a lot about Chopin's life. He died in Paris when he was only thirty-nine, and he was buried there, but his sister brought his heart back to Poland in an urn and put it in a church in Warsaw. That was because he was born in Poland, in a country village outside Warsaw.

Often we cooked together. Bubba always made soup—split pea soup, beetroot soup that was called borscht, and chicken soup. She made everything from scratch, and she was shocked when I told her I'd never had soup made from a whole chicken. I thought chicken soup always came in cans.

We made matzah balls to float in the soup, and the special bread called challah, and a dish with noodles called kugel. I was learning to cook a lot of new things, but what I liked most were the stories she told me while we were cooking.

Sarah said Zayde lived in another world, and Bubba's stories were about that other world. It was the old country where she and Zayde lived long ago before the war, and long before Sarah was born. That world no longer existed, but my grandmother made it so vivid that I could imagine it.

It was the old Jewish ghetto in Warsaw. There were shops and street vendors' stalls, special schools called yeshivas and synagogues. Old men in black hats and long coats argued back and forth about the Talmud, which were books of religious laws. Kids skipped rope in the streets and went to school. Bubba showed me pictures in the old books on the shelf in her bedroom. The pictures were black and white and yellow and the place looked gloomy, but when Bubba talked about it, I could practically hear the voices.

Some of the stories were scary, though. The scariest one was about the blood libel.

"Do you know what is libel?" she said.

"It's when people spread mean rumors about other people that aren't true."

The blood libel was a lie that was spread about the Jews. Someone who had a grudge would start a rumor that the Jews had killed a Christian child and used his blood to bake into matzah for Passover. Then all the people would rise up and kill the Jews.

"Did that happen in the old country?" I said.

"It happened everywhere. It happened in Russia, it happened in Spain, and it happened in Poland and in Arab countries, too."

"But that was a long time ago in the dark ages, wasn't it?" I said.

"Not so very long ago," Bubba said. "It happened in Poland even after the war, and after all that the Jews had suffered. It happened after the Warsaw ghetto had been destroyed, and most of the Jews killed. The few who managed to survive drifted back, but their neighbors had taken over their homes and stolen their possessions. So the old blood libel was revived as a means of getting rid of them."

"I hope my mother's stories don't bother you," Sarah said one day when we were waiting for my ferry.

"They don't," I said. "I like hearing about the old country."

"I grew up listening to those stories," she said. "They were what I heard instead of fairy tales."

"I like them a lot better than fairy tales," I said. "Didn't you?"

"No. They were all so sad. They depressed me then, and they depress me now."

"The only thing is," I said, "I want to know what happened to Bubba's sister, Rachel. Whenever I ask her, she says it's a long story and she'll tell me another time. But she says the same thing every time I ask, and I don't think she'll ever tell me."

"She'll tell you one of these days when she's ready."

"Why didn't she call you Rachel after her sister?" I said.

"That's a good question," she said. "I suppose when I was born she was hoping against hope that Rachel might still be alive. If she'd called me Rachel, it would have meant that she'd given up hope, because newborns are named only after the dear departed."

"And was Rachel still alive then?"

"As my mother says, it's a very long story," Sarah said.

"Did Rachel have a daughter?"

Sarah didn't say anything.

"Is that a long story, too?"

"Yes, Ellen, it is. And now there's the boarding announcement. Don't forget to give your father that package of papers, will you?"

After I got to the top of the gangplank I always looked back to see if Sarah was still there. She usually waited in her car to make sure I'd boarded. Then she started the car, turned around and headed back to the city.

When I got to the top of the gangplank on the day I'd asked her about my great-aunt Rachel, I saw that she was standing outside her car, leaning against the hood and watching me. She waved to me, and I waved back.

I thought that anyone watching us would think we were a normal mother and daughter. It gave me a good feeling, and I hoped she was starting to like me a little bit. I wondered if one day she might give me a big hug the way Bubba did when I arrived and when I left and sometimes in between.

I also wondered if I'd ever get to hear the long story about my great-aunt Rachel and find out what happened to her. I had a feeling it would have a very sad ending, like so many of Bubba's stories.

21

WHEN I WENT back and forth to Vancouver I felt like I was running a courier service. Gran sent knitting patterns to Bubba. Bubba sent recipes to Gran. Dad sent clippings from the local papers about the marina to Sarah. Sarah sent reports to Dad. They both sent books to each other.

They'd put together a ton of stuff showing the harm the marina development would cause. Even the twins knew the objections off by heart.

- The planned underground parking would be liable to flooding.
- The extra traffic would block the highways so that people traveling to the city would have a two-hour instead of a one-hour drive.

- The pollution from the extra boating traffic would kill the herring and salmon in the inlet, and there'd be no more commercial or sports fishing.
- Our water supply would give out. We'd have to bring in water from elsewhere. That would cause a huge increase in taxes and many locals would no longer be able to live here.

Dad said that if the development went through, it would be the end of Partridge Cove as we knew it. Sarah said there was so much evidence against the proposal that it couldn't possibly be approved.

But Dad said very few people could resist the propaganda machines. The developers had hired a public relations firm to draw up these beautiful sketches of the planned waterfront, showing walkways and smiling people pushing babies in strollers.

And the developers held open houses, which were like parties with free coffee and cookies, and everybody went and talked about how much they were looking forward to moving into luxury apartments that they thought would be selling for low prices.

I still walked along the beach and sat on my rock looking out at the inlet. But now I imagined

Partridge Cove disappearing the way Zayde's and Bubba's world had disappeared in Poland.

Instead of a quiet cove with a few sailboats and fishing boats bobbing on the water and seagulls flying overhead, there would be a row of steel and glass skyscrapers like the skyline of Vancouver. Partridge Cove would only exist in my head. Maybe I'd be telling stories about what the place was like once upon a time.

Often I listened in when Dad and Jake had conference calls with Sarah. They were preparing for the important next meeting when the community actually voted on the development.

"I predict the meeting will go well," Sarah said. "The material you've amassed contains undeniable evidence of the destructive effects of the development."

"I wouldn't count on it," Dad said. "Besides, even if this development is turned down, it's only a question of time before another developer comes along with a similar scheme."

"Then we'll fight it the same way," Sarah said.

"We'll get no support because everyone will be weary of the fight."

Mum used to say that Dad had an Eeyore personality, because he always looked on the gloomy side of things.

But even if he was pessimistic about the outcome of the meeting, all the preparations for it had cheered him up, just like Kelly had said they would. He was even looking better. He didn't wear sweaters with food stains on them any more, and he'd bought a snazzy new jacket and new shoes.

Kelly was the one person who wasn't excited about the meeting. She got crabby when Dad and Jake talked on the speakerphone with Sarah, or if either of them praised Sarah and said she had a good mind.

"She may have a good mind but she always looks a mess. With all her money, you'd think she'd make regular appointments at a hair salon and use a bit of make-up."

"She's too busy to sit in a hair salon for hours every week," I said.

It always bothered me when people criticized Sarah's hair, because mine was just like hers.

"No wonder she doesn't have a husband," Kelly said.

"If she doesn't have a husband, it's because she doesn't want one," Jake said.

That made Kelly really mad. She and Jake were always getting into fights these days. I was sure they'd break up pretty soon.

At the end of their phone calls, Dad and Jake

always warned Sarah about her safety. They told her to look out for signs that someone was following her when she was driving home from her office after working late. But Sarah just laughed.

"I've taken care of myself all these years and nothing's happened," she said.

In spite of Dad's predictions, the public hearing on the development turned out well. Sarah was right and he was wrong. The meeting lasted a long time. The developers went over the plans and showed the pictures and slides they'd shown before. They even added a new twist, saying they'd "gone green" with special toilets and stuff that would be good for the environment. Everybody goggled one last time at drawings of buildings that were supposed to have "affordable housing." They heard all about the great restaurant, the small art gallery, the hotel and all the beautiful condos with ocean views.

In the end, people were swayed by the reports of all the extra traffic and the water and sewage problems. They voted down the development by a very narrow margin.

We all walked home in a very cheerful mood. Dad was happier than anybody else.

"My faith in human nature and the power of reason has been restored," he said.

We couldn't wait to tell Sarah. She said she'd be working late and that she'd wait for our phone call. But when we called her office, no one answered.

"That's funny," Dad said. "Maybe she stepped out for a moment. Ellen, put the coffee pot on, and we'll call back in fifteen minutes."

"I don't see why I should make coffee for everybody," I said. "I don't even drink it."

"Quit arguing and just do as I say for once," Dad said.

"I'll do it," Kelly said. "I might as well do something while we're all hanging around waiting to talk to Sarah."

After fifteen minutes, Dad called back, but Sarah was still not answering her phone. He called her condo but she wasn't there, either.

"Maybe she went out on a date," Kelly said. "I'm sure she doesn't tell you two about her love life. Some men like rich women, whatever they look like."

"Do you have her cell number?" Jake asked, but neither Dad nor I did.

We were all beginning to get worried. Then I had the idea of calling Bubba's house. Sarah didn't usually go over there on weekdays, but I thought Bubba might know where she was.

The phone rang and rang and finally someone answered, but the person didn't speak English.

"That's Rosa," I said. "She sometimes comes in to help Bubba with Zayde."

Rosa knew me, but we hadn't talked to each other much because she didn't have many English words. But I spoke to her very slowly and asked her if she knew where Sarah was. I caught the words "hospital" and "crash" and something about a car going very fast. The others were crowding around, trying to hear.

"Rosa, was it a car accident?" I said.

"Car, yes," she said. "Big car. Big light. Go fast. Much noise. Zzzoom."

"I think it was a car accident," I told the others. "Sarah's in the hospital and Bubba's there with her. I don't know if they're both hurt. Rosa must be staying with Zayde."

"Ask her which hospital," Dad said. His face was white and his hands were shaking.

"I'm going over there," Jake said, when I put the phone down. "If I leave right away I'll just catch the last ferry."

"I'll come with you," Dad said. "Kelly can stay here and see to things."

"No way I'm staying with the kids," Kelly said. "I'm out of here. And if you go chasing off to Vancouver after that woman, that's the end of it. I'm finished with you!" she said to Jake.

Then she got her coat and stomped out. So Dad stayed with us. Jake took Dad's car to the ferry. He promised to call us the moment he got there and found out what had happened.

After Jake left, Dad sat staring into space. After all the excitement of the meeting, he'd gone back to the way he was just after Mum died. Instead of celebrating, everything was all upset and awful again.

I thought Dad would send me off to bed, but he seemed to have forgotten about us kids. The twins got some milk and then went down to their room.

I flopped down on the sofa and started to think about all the times I'd thought about girls who had real mothers. I'd envied the ones who had the same talents, like Jenny and Anne with their art, and Dimsie and Catriona with their music. I used to wish I had a mother like that.

I didn't know how lucky I was having a nice mother I could tell my troubles to.

I had a talented mother now, but she sure wasn't interested in hearing about my problems. And there were a lot of things I didn't like about her. She wasn't very friendly, and she wasn't very nice to Bubba. The only person she really liked was Zayde.

But in a way, Sarah and I were alike. We had the same hair and eyes. Dad often said I had a sharp tongue and a quick temper, and so did Sarah. Also she argued a lot just like me, only nobody told her to stop the way Dad and Higg did to me.

"Sarah has the spirit of contention," Dad always said, as if it was a good thing. That made me mad because it was a double standard.

Then I thought about the last time she took me to the ferry and I'd looked back at her car. She'd been standing outside and she waved at me just as if we were a normal mother and daughter.

I must have fallen asleep as I was thinking about Sarah waving to me across the strip of water.

22

IN MY DREAM a phone was ringing and someone was pulling at my arm. Only suddenly it wasn't a dream. Dad was sitting on the edge of the sofa and telling me to wake up.

"What time is it?" I said. It was still dark out.

"It's early," Dad said. "Listen, Ellen, Sarah's not hurt. She's fine. We misunderstood. It's Zayde who had an accident. He fell down and then he had a heart attack. The car that Rosa was talking about was the ambulance that rushed him to the hospital. Sarah wants you to go over there immediately."

"Why?" I said.

"I don't know," Dad said. "I honestly don't. Maybe your grandmother wants you there."

"Okay," I said. "How will I get there?"

"She's sending a floatplane. It's already on its way."

The next hour was very confused. Dad and I hurried down to the marina, and in the distance we saw the floatplane, like a big bird. It came nearer and nearer and finally came down on the water. A man stepped out and pulled me inside and then it took off again.

It was very strange and beautiful. The sun was beginning to rise and it was red and bright and shining behind the mountains. As I looked, it rose above the hills and shone on the water. When I looked down, I saw all the islands in the gulf looking green and small, like lily pads. Then the skyline of Vancouver appeared with its row of skyscrapers. Beyond them, the hills were dotted with houses, one above the other like a crowd of people all straining to see the water.

"You ever been in a floatplane before?" the pilot asked me.

"No," I said.

"Some guy's supposed to meet you at the harbor," he said.

For a moment my heart did a flip-flop. I remembered how worried Jake and Dad had been about someone stalking Sarah. Suppose this was all a trick and they were about to kidnap me and hold me for ransom?

But before I could worry about that for long, the plane went down on the water, and soon a dock appeared. And at the end of the dock was Jake.

"We have to hurry, Ellen," he said. "I have to get you to the hospital as fast as I can."

"Can we stop for something to eat? I haven't had any breakfast."

"Sorry! There's no time to spare. Your zayde . . ."

Jake skidded into the hospital parking lot and rushed me into the hospital. We hurried down a long corridor that smelled of disinfectant, up an elevator, down another corridor and stopped at a nursing station where a nurse sat behind a desk with a vase of pink and white carnations on it.

"Go right in, they're waiting for you," the nurse said, and she pointed to a door down the hall.

Zayde was lying in bed with his eyes closed. There was a tube running from a plastic bag on a metal pole and sticking into his arm. Both his arms were lying on top of the sheets.

Bubba and Sarah were sitting on opposite sides of the bed. They both got up when I walked in.

"Rachel's come to see you," Sarah said very loudly to Zayde.

It was the first time she'd ever called me Rachel, and I wondered if she was mixed up. She cranked the bed a bit to raise Zayde's shoulders up. His eyes fluttered open and then settled on my face. He stared at me and said something I didn't understand.

"Tell him you forgive him," Sarah said.

"What for?"

"Just say it!" She took my hand and put it over his. His hand was very cold.

"I forgive you, Zayde," I said. He showed no sign that he heard me.

"Say it again," Sarah said. So I said it again, louder.

This time he closed his eyes again and his mouth moved slightly. He seemed to be trying to smile. Then all by himself he lifted his other hand and put it on top of mine. I felt as if my hand was in a sandwich between his two cold ones.

Sarah and Bubba looked at each other and nodded. They seemed relieved. Zayde's skin was like yellow paper, and the veins stood up like blue worms.

Quite a long time seemed to pass, but I didn't like to take my hand away. I was wondering what to do next when my stomach growled very loudly.

"I'm a little hungry," I said. "I haven't had anything to eat."

Sarah very gently lifted Zayde's hand up and set my hand free. Then she took me outside to where Jake was chatting with the nurse.

"Jake, could I ask one more favor?" Sarah said.

"Anything, Sarah," Jake said.

"Ellen's famished. Could you take her down to the cafeteria and get her some breakfast? And then you'd better get back to Partridge Cove. David will be needing his car."

"Shall I take her back with me?"

"No. Get her back here as soon as possible in case Zayde asks for her again."

The cafeteria smelled of frying bacon and potatoes. A man in a white hat was cooking eggs and flipping them over on a big hotplate. The smell of the hospital corridors was still in my nose and made me feel a bit sick.

As soon as I saw the food, I lost my appetite.

"Just get some juice and some toast then," Jake said.

He got coffee and a doughnut for himself and carried everything on a tray over to a table by the window. I nibbled at the toast and looked at the trees in pots in a little courtyard outside.

"Kelly's really mad at you," I said.

"I guess," Jake said. He didn't seem too upset.

"Will you get together with Sarah?" I said.

"I don't think Sarah would go for someone like me," Jake said. "She's more your dad's type."

"My dad?" I said.

"Look, finish up that toast and I'll take you back to Zayde's room. He's probably asking for you again."

So we went back along the smelly corridors to Zayde's room.

23

ZAYDE DIDN'T ASK for me again. He died late that afternoon. I thought about all the people who had crowded around him on Rosh Hashanah outside the synagogue. He hadn't been written down in the Book of Life, after all.

It was dark when the three of us went back to Bubba's house. The doctor had given her a sleeping pill because she hadn't slept at all the night before, but before she closed her bedroom door, she worried about making us something to eat. Sarah told her she'd fix something for herself and me.

She opened the fridge and looked inside. It was full of food, but she just shook her head.

"Would you like me to make some matzah brei?" I said.

"Can you do that?" she said. "It's about the only thing I could face just now."

"Bubba showed me how," I said. "It's easy."

I got out the eggs and found a box of matzah. I took out two of the big square crackers and ran water over them. When they were soft, I crumbled them into bits. Then I beat the eggs well, added some milk, mixed it all together and cooked it in a frying pan on the top of the stove.

Sarah sat at the table watching me.

"My mother used to make that when I was a kid," she said.

We sat at the table across from each other. It was okay to drink milk with eggs, so I poured myself a glass. Sarah put a bottle of wine on the table and poured herself some. She seemed to feel better after she'd eaten.

"Sarah," I said. "Was it Zayde who made you give me up for adoption? Is that why I had to say I'd forgiven him?"

"No, of course not," she said. "I didn't tell anybody in the family about your birth. I got a summer job outside the city and didn't see them for months. If Zayde and my mother had known, you wouldn't have been adopted. They'd never have allowed it."

Ever since I'd found Sarah, I'd had a ton of questions. I wondered if I'd ever get up the nerve to ask why she put me up for adoption. Now it seemed like the question was floating in the air between us, but I still couldn't say it.

Then Sarah suddenly put down her glass.

"I grew up in this house," she said. "It was very crowded, with Zayde, my father, my mother and myself. It was a small house full of anger, and they never stopped arguing."

"What did they argue about?" I said.

"Everything. They fought about religious observances, what kind of food to buy, which food was too expensive and too extravagant, whether they should buy a car or a piano. They quarreled about me—whether they could afford music lessons, which I didn't want in the first place. They'd come to this city as refugees. They arrived with not much more than the clothes they wore, a bag of old photographs and those candlesticks you see on the table. And a menorah, of course. Yet my mother had to have a piano, even though it meant paying for it in installments for years. There was never enough money, and when there isn't enough money, the things to quarrel about are endless."

"Did your mum and dad fight, too?"

"Sometimes. But my dad was too discouraged and defeated to have much energy left for fighting. Mainly it was my mother and Zayde."

"If they fought so much, why did Zayde stay here with them?"

"Where else could he go? He was old and sick even then. And he'd suffered so much. Besides, it wasn't that simple. They made each other angry and they fought, but at the same time they loved each other. Your family's so normal, I suppose it's hard for to you understand how people in a family can love and hate each other at the same time."

"No, it's not," I said.

"Anyway, I didn't even have my own bedroom or any place I could call my own. Zayde was my only comfort, and I suppose I was his. We walked, went to the park, and even when we didn't talk, we were happy in each other's company. I had no friends my own age. He was everything to me.

"After my father died, I slept on a pallet in my mother's room. I hated it. I decided very early that I never wanted to be part of a family again. A family to me meant too many people all jammed up together in a house too small for them. I didn't want to get married. And I didn't want to be worried about money every time I went to the grocery store, and frightened every time the mail came in case there were bills I couldn't pay. So I got out of there as soon as I could. I escaped."

"How did you do that?"

"I worked very hard in school. I won a full scholarship to university. I worked every summer to earn money."

"What kind of work?"

"All kinds. I cleaned houses and babysat. I worked in fast-food restaurants. Then I won a scholarship to law school. I was very determined not to let anything stand in my way."

I guess I was something that stood in her way.

Neither of us said anything for quite a long time. She was lost in thought. I was just wondering if I should clear away the dishes when I thought of something else.

"Sarah," I said. "If Zayde didn't know about me being adopted, what was I supposed to forgive him for?"

"That's a very different story," Sarah said. She was quiet for a while. Then she poured herself another glass of wine. "It's the story of my aunt Rachel, your great-aunt."

"It's a long story, isn't it?" I said.

"Yes," she said. "It is long in many ways. You know, Zayde was very confused, and in his confusion, he mixed you up with Rachel. You look so much like her."

"What happened to her?"

"Well, it was a very long time ago in Poland. This

was before the war and before...well, before. My grandparents—your great-grandparents—lived in Warsaw. They were very devout Jews, and there was a custom...It was a very cruel custom..."

"What was it?"

"If any of the daughters of the family married out of the faith...that is, if they married someone who wasn't a Jew, they were cast out of the family. The family even published a notice of their death in the paper, because, in effect, that daughter was dead as far as the family was concerned. It was worse than being dead because the dead are remembered."

"And that's what happened to Rachel?"

"Your great-aunt was a brilliant pianist, and she studied at the Chopin Academy in Warsaw. There she fell in love with her teacher, who was a gentile. They were a perfect couple—handsome, gifted, and in love. And they decided, in spite of the opposition of both their families, that they would marry...so they did."

"What happened after that?"

"They left Warsaw together to start a new life. Zayde put a notice of Rachel's death in the paper, and none of the family ever saw her again. My mother remembers Rachel coming into her bedroom in the early morning when she was sleeping.

She woke her up, gave her a necklace she always wore, and told her goodbye. My mother never heard or saw anything of her sister ever again. Her name was never mentioned in the household. My mother never forgave Zayde for that."

"Was he ever sorry for what he did?"

"Well, he was stubborn. He would never admit that he did anything wrong. At least not until the very end of his life."

"And then he did?"

"Don't you see, Ellen? When he asked you to forgive him, he thought he was asking Rachel. That was his way of admitting that this terrible thing he did was wrong. It must have been preying on his mind for years, but he was too proud to admit it. You see that, don't you?"

"I didn't before, but I do now," I said. "Poor Zayde."

"What you said allowed your great-grandfather to die in peace."

"There's something else I don't get," I said.

"What's that?" She sounded very tired.

"Why didn't Bubba look for Rachel when she was grown up?"

"By then it was too late. The Holocaust had happened. The whole world had changed. The Jews of Poland had disappeared, many of them without a trace.

"After she came to Canada, my mother tried to find out what had happened to her sister. She sought out other refugees, contacted as many survivors as she could. One survivor remembered that a woman very much like Rachel played the piano for the opera that was performed at the concentration camp outside Prague. But we know the composer and many who took part in *Brundibar* were eventually shipped off to Auschwitz and murdered.

"Another survivor told her that Rachel had joined the Jewish partisans who made camps deep in the forests of Poland. There were many such camps, some with whole families in them. Some of the fugitives carried out nighttime raids on the Nazi units that occupied the small towns nearby. The Nazis penetrated the forests, tracked down the partisans and murdered them — men, women and children."

"What a sad story," I said.

"You'll learn all about those horrors one day, but this is not the time. We've both had enough sorrow for one day. You should get some sleep."

It was too late to drive back to Sarah's condo so we made up a bed for me on the couch in the living room.

"Ellen," she said after I was tucked up, "you've had a pretty happy childhood, haven't you?"

"Fairly good," I said.

"Your father's a very kind man, isn't he?"

"Yes."

I had a lot of complaints about Dad and the way he treated me worse than the twins, but after what I'd just heard, he seemed okay. I couldn't imagine him ever getting so mad at me that he'd put a notice in the paper saying I was dead.

"Where will you sleep?" I said. There was only Zayde's room, and I thought it would be very creepy to sleep in there.

"Don't worry about me," she said. "I have a lot to think about before I go to bed. Sleep well, Ellen."

For a moment I thought she was going to hug me, but she just pulled the blanket over me and patted me on the shoulder.

I had a lot to think about, too, and I didn't think I'd go to sleep for a long time. Some of my questions had been answered, but I had tons more I wanted to ask.

And there was still one big question. I wondered if I'd ever get up the courage to ask Sarah about my birth father.

24

IT SEEMED LIKE I had just got home when I had to turn around and go back to Zayde's funeral.

"In my day children didn't attend funerals," Gran said. "And this is so soon after her mother...well...it's bound to be upsetting for Ellen."

"Grandma Rebecca wants me there," I said, "so I'm going."

"She wants you there too often in my opinion," Gran said. "You neglect your school work and your music and your chores around the house. And you come back exhausted. You have circles under your eyes most of the time."

"I've decided to drive Ellen over," Dad said. "I'll go to the funeral with her. It will be easier on her if I'm there to provide some moral support."

When we got to Vancouver, we drove straight to Bubba's house. This time she wasn't looking out the window, and it was Sarah who opened the door. Instead of a pantsuit and flat shoes, she was wearing a black dress and black stockings. And she'd put some stuff on her hair so that it wasn't sticking out all over the place. She was also wearing glasses for the first time. Behind them her eyes were red.

I was wearing the clothes Sarah had bought me for Rosh Hashanah. I wanted to see what I looked like but I couldn't, because all the mirrors in the house were covered up with sheets.

Dad was wearing his best dark suit that he hardly ever wore, and he'd bought a new white shirt and a black tie. Bubba gave him a yarmulke to wear to the synagogue. It covered up his bald patch perfectly. He looked quite handsome, actually.

My grandmother said she was going to make a cut on everybody's clothes—even on Dad's and mine, because we were family now. It was an old custom from the days when mourners rent their clothes up in grief.

"Surely we're not going to do that?" Sarah said.

"Zayde would have wanted us to."

"But you always say the old customs have no place in the new world!" Sarah said.

"Your zayde was never a part of the new world." She wiped her eyes.

"Oh, very well. I'll do it, then, if it means so much to you," Sarah said. "I suppose it's all right to use scissors."

Dad looked a bit freaked out at the thought of having his clothes cut up.

"Don't worry, David," Sarah said. "I won't inflict a great deal of damage on your good clothes."

Even though she'd been crying, she smiled when she said it.

"I'm not worried," he said.

She held his tie to one side, and made a tiny cut in the front of his shirt.

I was a bit nervous when Sarah made a small cut in the front of my jacket, but it hardly showed. She was going to hand the scissors to me, but Dad stepped forward and took them from her.

"May I?" he said, looking at the lapel of her dress.

"It has to be on the left side nearest the heart," she said. Her shoes had high heels and she wobbled a bit in them.

Dad kept fumbling with the scissors like an idiot. Instead of watching what he was doing, he was looking at Sarah's face like he'd never seen her before. She put her hand on his shoulder and they started to giggle.

"This is not the time for laughing," my grandmother said. "You should be ashamed of yourselves." They both looked like kids who'd been caught doing something wrong. Dad coughed and apologized.

The funeral was a lot different from Mum's memorial service. There were no photographs of Zayde when he was a young man. Nobody called it a celebration and said he'd had a good life. It was very solemn and I liked the chants and the prayers. I was surprised that the synagogue was full of people, and the first person I saw when I walked in was Spotz. After the service, Zayde's coffin was carried out and we went to a cemetery.

When we walked into the cemetery, the traffic noises of the city were faint in the distance, and it was very quiet. Even the trees were dark and gloomy, and no birds were singing. We went slowly down a path between graves. Every time the procession behind Zayde's coffin stopped, I looked at the grave stones. There were Stars of David and menorahs and Hebrew letters and numbers on them. The numbers were dates in the Jewish calendar.

The grave was a deep square hole, and the men lowered the coffin into it. My grandmother had put some of Zayde's books in a little bag, and she put them in the grave with him. Then the men took a shovel and put some of the dirt back in the grave. When I heard the dirt hit the coffin, I suddenly went cold. Sarah must have gone cold, too, because she started to tremble. Dad put his hand on her arm to steady her, and she said the prayer for the dead in a very low voice. I remembered the time Zayde asked if I was a kaddish, and I wished I knew the words so I could say them with her.

Then we went back to the house. It was very crowded with people I didn't know. They would come over for seven days and it was called sitting shiva. There was tons of food at the house and I was very hungry. Nobody offered me anything to eat, so I went over to the table and helped myself. I couldn't talk to Bubba because she was sitting on a stool with a lot of old ladies crowding around her. Nobody paid any attention to me. Dad was supposed to be giving me moral support, but the one he was really looking after was Sarah.

She sat on the couch with Dad beside her. He asked if he could get her something and she said she'd like a glass of wine. He brought the wine and a small plate with some food on it.

"You should try to eat something," he said. He even stuck a bite of cheese on a fork and tried to put it in her mouth, which looked stupid.

I was just wishing we could leave when Dad turned to me.

"I'm going to drive Sarah home," he said.

"Why can't she drive herself?" I said.

"She's very upset and in no condition to get behind the wheel."

"Can I come?"

"No, you wait here. I'll be back very shortly."

But he wasn't back shortly. It seemed like hours, and when he finally turned up, he said we'd better hurry if we wanted to catch the ferry.

We hardly spoke on the ferry home, and as soon as we walked into our house, he said he was going to call Sarah to let her know we'd got back safely.

"Why wouldn't we get back safely?" I said.

"Well, I also want to see how she is. This was a sad day for her. She was very attached to Zayde and she didn't look at all well."

"Bubba didn't look at all well, either," I said. "You should call her."

"I'll let you do that," he said.

But I didn't. I just went off to bed.

25

DAD WOULDN'T GO down the garden after Mum died, so I was quite surprised when he turned up at Somecot one afternoon.

"May I come in?" he said.

"Sure."

When Jenny comes I usually offer to make her some hot chocolate or something, but I was still mad about the way Dad had treated me after Zayde's funeral.

He looked around as if he'd never seen the place before. Then he spotted the photos of Mum and my great-aunt Rachel side by side in their matching frames on the wall.

He went over and stood looking at them for quite a long time.

"It's kind of a mess in here," I said. "I've been spending so much time in Vancouver lately."

"Ah, yes, Vancouver," he said. "That's what I came to talk to you about. More or less."

He looked a bit doubtfully at my beanbag chair so I got off my desk chair and sat on the beanbag. He sat on my desk chair. He leaned forward and looked down at the floor between his feet. He seemed to be having trouble getting started.

"You remember when Mum died…?" he said.

"Of course I remember."

"Yes. Well, after she died I found a letter she left me. She wrote it just before she went into hospital that last time."

I didn't say anything.

"She knew she wouldn't be with us much longer. And I suppose she was wondering what our lives would be like after she was gone. She said she didn't like to think of me going through life alone. She said she hoped I'd eventually find a companion to share my life with. Someone who would also be a good friend to you children."

"So?"

"Well, I think I have found someone…"

"It's Sarah, isn't it?"

He looked up in surprise.

"How did you guess?"

It was so obvious. Everybody knows, I wanted to say—Jake, Kelly, probably the whole of Partridge Cove. I'd known ever since I saw him look at Sarah when he made the cut in her dress before Zayde's funeral.

"Sarah doesn't want to be your companion, does she?" I said.

"Well, why not? I'm not a monster, am I?"

You're a cranky old man with a bunch of kids she can't stand, I thought.

"You're a lot older than she is," I said.

"Eight years isn't a lot older."

"I guess not." Spotz was three grades ahead of me in school, but he didn't seem a whole lot older.

"Anyway, what I came to tell you is that when you go over to see Rebecca next weekend, I'll be going with you. To see Sarah. And she'll be coming over here some weekend in the future."

"Where will she stay?"

"We'll work that out later."

"She isn't going to be a good friend to the twins," I said. "She can't stand them. She calls them the gruesome twosome."

"She does? Well, she isn't used to children."

"She isn't going to get used to them," I said. "The more she sees of them the more disgusted she'll be."

"Look, Ellen, we have to give things time to settle. People do change, you know. The twins won't always be the rambunctious pair they are now. In fact, they're already showing signs of maturity."

"Oh, really?" I said. "I haven't noticed any."

"Brian tells me their teacher is very pleased with their progress in school."

What about my progress, I thought. I'll bet Higg had a lot to say about that. I hadn't done well all year. I never got my work in on time any more, and my grades had gone way down. I wouldn't be surprised if I failed and had to go to summer school or repeat the year. Maybe they'd given me up as a lost cause.

"We've all changed in the past year," Dad said. "Sarah herself has changed. I've changed. You've changed."

"Me?"

"You may not have realized it, but you've grown up. Suffering a great loss has that effect. We all suffered a great loss and it's changed and aged every one of us."

It was the first time Dad and I had really talked since Mum died. Suddenly I didn't want him to leave, even though it was getting cold in Somecot.

"Would you like some tea?" I said. "I have lemon or black currant."

"You can make tea down here?"

"Yes, don't you remember when Gran gave me that electric kettle?"

"I'll take the lemon tea, please."

So I gave him a mug of lemon tea and a shortbread cookie.

"I'll forego the cookie," he said.

I'd noticed he was dressing better and watching his weight these days.

"This is quite a cozy little nest you have here," he said. "It's a bit chilly, though. You could do with a heater. We'll have to see about getting you one."

"Dad," I said. "What did you think when you read what Mum said about finding a companion?"

"I thought it was inconceivable," he said. "I couldn't imagine such a thing ever happening in a million years."

"Mum wrote me a letter, too," I said.

"She did?"

"She said she hoped I'd find my birth mother and that we'd become friends."

"So that was the reason you started searching. I wondered at the time…"

"Do you think Mum knew how it would turn out?"

"I don't think she could have foreseen exactly how things would turn out," Dad said. "She hoped we'd rebuild our lives, and she was giving us a friendly little push in that direction."

Neither of us said anything for a while. Dad put his tea down, polished the steam off his glasses and wiped his eyes. I was getting that lump back in my throat, when suddenly a great noisy clatter broke out back at the house.

It was the bell on the deck—not just the one or two rings that Dad gives it when he needs me in the kitchen—but enough of a racket to disturb the entire neighborhood.

"Good heavens," Dad said. "Just look at the time, and we've not done anything about supper."

So we left the mugs and rushed up to the house. I was thinking I'd fix some grilled cheese sandwiches and open a can of soup. But when we got there Tim was heating up a pot of vegetarian chili on the stove and Toby was cutting up a baguette he'd brought from the bakery. There was a plate of carrots and celery and jicama already cut up on the table.

"It would be nice if we got a bit of help around here once in while," Tim said.

"Yeah, in the garden, too," Toby said.

He looked at the schedule with a list of our garden chores that we'd put under a magnet on the fridge. I hadn't done mine for ages.

"Thanks for picking up the leaves and rotten apples in Mum's garden," I said.

"That's okay," Toby said. "But if you wouldn't mind clearing up after supper, we've got a ton of homework."

"I'll help," Dad said.

"Dad," I said after the twins had gone off to do their homework, "when are you going to tell the twins about you and Sarah?"

"As soon as I brace myself for the inevitable questions and irreverent remarks," he said.

"What do you think Gran will say when you tell her?" I said.

"It doesn't bear thinking about," he said.

I actually felt sorry for him.

"Mum always said if you want to get Gran to agree to something, all you have to do is convince her it was her idea in the first place."

"That might be rather difficult in this case."

"Mum was usually right about things, wasn't she?" I said.

"Yes, she was."

26

MY GRANDMOTHER HELD a Seder to celebrate the first night of Passover. It's a very special dinner, and she even has a separate set of dishes that she uses only at Passover. All the week before, she and Rosa had been cleaning the house from top to bottom.

Bubba invited Gran and Dad and the twins because we are all family now. She also invited Jenny because it is the custom to invite a guest from outside the family. The only one who didn't accept was Gran.

"I didn't think religious ceremonies were much in your line, either," she said to Dad.

"It is an ancient tradition," he said, "and I'm honored to be included."

"I thought you were skeptical of ancient traditions and rituals."

"There is a time to suspend skepticism," Dad said. "It will be good for us all to learn some Jewish history."

"And how will they feel at having a non-believer in their midst on such an occasion?"

"Ellen tells me that the performance of good deeds is valued as much as religious observances in the Jewish faith."

"It's called a mitzvah when you do a good deed for others," I said.

"Oh, is it?" Gran said. "And when was the last time you did such a deed, David?"

"When I picked up that box of live crickets at the pet shop in the city and brought them home for the twins," Dad said. "I should think that counts as a good deed by anybody's standards."

"No, it doesn't," I said. "A mitzvah has to be done with a joyous heart, and you didn't do it with a joyous heart. Just the opposite."

"Well, I shall not be joining you, but I shall send Rebecca a box of my shortbread," Gran said.

"Bread of any kind is forbidden on Passover," I said. "Only matzah's allowed."

"Then I shall send her a card," Gran said. "She sent me a very nice Easter card. We've become quite good friends."

"And so have Sarah and I," Dad said. "You were right, Mother, when you encouraged me to get to know Sarah better."

"I don't recall doing anything of the kind."

"No? Well, you have a tendency to underestimate the value of your own good advice."

"I suppose I have. That's because it isn't always appreciated in this house."

"In this instance it is and I'm grateful for it," Dad said. "Sarah has proved to be a good friend to all of us, just as you predicted."

"Sarah's cool," Tim said.

She'd chartered a floatplane to take us all over to the mainland and bring us back.

"We're the only kids in our class who get to go to Vancouver in a floatplane," Toby said.

"I'm thinking of making a new will and leaving her my watch," Tim said.

"She's already got a very expensive watch," I said.

"Not one where the face lights up in the dark."

Jenny and I didn't go with the others in the floatplane. We went over the day before on the ferry. We helped Bubba with the cooking and then we spent the night at Sarah's condo.

The Seder is quite a complicated meal with a lot of different dishes. It celebrates the time the

Children of Israel finally got away from Egypt where they'd been kept as slaves. Bubba told us the story while we made the gefilte fish.

At first the pharaoh wouldn't agree to free them, even though Moses kept saying, "Let my people go." Then ten plagues rained down on the Egyptians. These were plagues of frogs and bugs and boils and hailstones, and diseases that the cattle came down with.

The worst plague was when all the first-born sons of the Egyptians died, but the Angel of Death passed over the sons of the Israelites. That was the last straw for the pharaoh. So he finally got worn down and let them head off to the Promised Land. They got out of there so fast that they didn't even wait for the bread they needed for the journey to rise. That's why we eat unleavened bread or matzah on Passover.

All the food we prepared had a special meaning. There were bitter herbs for the bitterness of being slaves, and fruit paste with chopped nuts and apples for the mortar that the Jews used to make the bricks stick together. Usually there's lamb because the Children of Israel put the blood of a lamb on the doorposts so the Angel of Death would know which houses to pass over. But Bubba was cooking chicken because I don't like lamb.

At the beginning of the meal the youngest kid asks four questions, so Tim and Toby took turns asking them. Bubba had given me a book called a Haggadah so that I could teach them the questions. The first two were —

"Why is this night different from all other nights?"

and

"Why do we eat unleavened bread?"

We already know the answers, but we ask them anyway because it's a ritual. What Tim really wanted to ask about were the plagues. Anyway, he did what he was told, and we all enjoyed sitting around the table in the candlelight and hearing the story unfold.

There was a special place set in case Elijah, the Prophet of Peace, arrived. The door was left open for him, and a glass of wine by his place. The twins were disappointed that he didn't come, but Bubba said that there was always next year.

It was a good thing that Sarah had chartered the floatplane, because it was a very long meal and we were very tired by the end of it. We all squeezed into Sarah's car and she drove us down to the waterfront. It was dark when the floatplane came down at the Partridge Cove marina, and the sky was full of stars. We walked up the hill, dropped Jenny off at her house, and then went on home.

Even though it was late, I didn't go to bed right away. Instead I went down to Somecot to write to Mum.

Dear Mum,

You remember I said you were wrong about my birth mother becoming my friend. Well, now I think you were right after all. She is getting to like me. She and Dad are good friends, and even Gran is getting used to her. She said the other day that Dad could do worse for a companion.

But my really good new friend is my Grandma Rebecca. I wish you could meet her. I've told her all about you and she feels she knows you. She's given me a yahrzeit candle and I'm going to light it on the day you left us and let it burn for twenty-four hours from sunset to sunset.

We've kept your garden just the way you like it. It's all cleaned up and the spring flowers are blooming. We have a schedule on the fridge and we take turns watering and weeding. The only time the twins missed out on the watering was when Primrose was shedding her skin and they didn't want to miss it.

I can't think of anything else so I will say bye for now.

Love,

Ellen

P.S. I miss you every day, especially when I come home from school.

JOAN GIVNER, a former university English professor, is an author and book reviewer who has written a dozen books of biography, autobiography and fiction, including *Katherine Anne Porter: A Life* and the novels *Half Known Lives* and *Playing Sarah Bernhardt*. She has written three previous Ellen books—*Ellen Fremedon*, *Ellen Fremedon, Journalist* and *Ellen Fremedon, Volunteer*—which have been nominated for several awards. Joan lives on Vancouver Island in Mill Bay, a small seaside town not unlike Partridge Cove.

ALSO AVAILABLE BY JOAN GIVNER

ELLEN FREMEDON

To fight boredom one lazy summer, Ellen Fremedon decides to write a novel. It will be a long one with many chapters and a plot full of mystery and intrigue. But when an urgent, real-life plot begins to unfold right in her sleepy seaside village, Ellen must find the time to be both a writer, and an environmental activist.

Paperback $8.95 CAN / $5.95 US
ISBN-13: 978-0-88899-640-4
ISBN-10: 0-88899-640-3

ELLEN FREMEDON, JOURNALIST

Ellen Fremedon and her best friend, Jenny, decide to publish a newspaper — a paper that will, unlike so many others, be completely truthful and free of mistakes. But publishing a newspaper isn't as easy as it seems, and being an investigative reporter in a small community like Partridge Cove is a profession full of unexpected pitfalls, especially when it comes time to investigate the mysterious stranger who moves in next door.

Paperback $9.95 CAN / $6.95 US
ISBN-13: 978-0-88899-691-6
ISBN-10: 0-88899-691-8

ELLEN FREMEDON, VOLUNTEER

Bored, grumpy and friendless, Ellen Fremedon faces a summer full of extra chores and a dreary volunteer gig at the local retirement home. That's where she meets Mr. Martin — a blind, rude old man who is even crankier than Ellen — and her summer begins to take some unexpected turns.

Paperback $9.95 CAN / $8.95 US
ISBN-13: 978-0-88899-744-9
ISBN-10: 0-88899-744-2